“Me[illegible]

She raised her glass, repeating the toast as a log settled on the grate. Flames leaped up, etching his features ruddy-bronze, and through some strange alchemy of wine and music, he seemed to radiate heat and light.

It might have been an optical illusion, a capricious trick of light, but she took it as an omen.

She wanted to make love with him, but she refused to romanticize her feelings.

Love was a pipe dream for poets and paperback novels. It was fine for old Doris Day movies and for lovable people like her parents. But she had stopped expecting to be loved when she'd given up believing in Santa Claus, and since then she'd got along without love very well, thank you.

All she wanted was for Jonathan to hold her close. Just for tonight.

ABOUT THE AUTHOR

Robin Francis read hundreds of romance novels before attempting to write one herself. Despite her passion for baseball, Robin began working on her first book during a World Series, and found her new hobby so addicting that she has been a happily published author ever since. This is her thirteenth romance novel, and her third for Harlequin American Romance.

Books by Robin Francis

HARLEQUIN AMERICAN ROMANCE

38–MEMORIES OF LOVE
88–SEASON OF DREAMS

Taking a Chance

Robin Francis

Harlequin Books

TORONTO • NEW YORK • LONDON
AMSTERDAM • PARIS • SYDNEY • HAMBURG
STOCKHOLM • ATHENS • TOKYO • MILAN

Published July 1988

First printing May 1988

ISBN 0-373-16253-7

Printed in U.S.A.

Chapter One

The redhead moved into the studio the Friday before Christmas. Jonathan didn't actually meet her till the following Monday, but he knew she was a redhead because he caught a glimpse of her through the second-floor window when he got home from work. He knew she was a flake by the housewarming party that lasted the better part of the next twenty-four hours.

As usual, Jonathan had brought home a briefcase full of paperwork. He had intended to spend the weekend planning investment strategies that would permit his clients to take advantage of changes in the tax laws which would go into effect the first of the year. Unfortunately, he had installed his computer terminal in the dining alcove, directly beneath the main room of the studio, and the glass-on-brass chiming of the chandelier told him of the party's progress.

By nine o'clock the noise had grown from minor distraction to major irritant. The ceiling vibrated to the beat of "Jingle Bell Rock." The walls shook with laughter. The floor quaked from the heavy footsteps that galloped through the building's vestibule, along the corridor and up the stairs.

About ten-thirty a trio of latecomers pounded at his door and asked for directions to Paulette's. Jonathan might have told them where he wished they'd go if he hadn't taken a certain pride in keeping his temper in check. He gritted his teeth, pointed toward the stairs and said, "Second floor, first door on the right."

Over the next couple of hours this scene was repeated until, fed up, Jonathan ignored the interruptions.

By the small hours of Saturday morning, his estimate of his upstairs neighbor had reached a new low. Not only was she an inconsiderate kook, but she seemed to have acquired her guest list from Rent-a-Jock. Without exception, her visitors were muscle-bound types who apparently couldn't count to two.

Not that he didn't keep fit himself. Staying in shape physically gave him a sense of well-being, increased his stamina and enhanced his powers of concentration. Logic dictated he follow an exercise program that included an early morning jog and weight training three times a week, and although the comings and goings at the party kept him from sleeping well that night, Saturday morning was no exception.

He was awake at seven, and by seven-fifteen he was dressed in thermal underwear, a sweat suit, ski cap and running shoes. Quiet pervaded the building as he left his apartment and let himself out the street door.

Evidently the redhead was getting her beauty sleep.

Thus far he had behaved with admirable restraint, but as he stepped onto the porch, he yielded to impulse and let the door slam behind him. The sound echoed through the hallway and up the stairwell like rifle fire, but he didn't expect the gesture to accomplish anything.

Chances were the lady in the studio slept right through it. He also realized that two rudenesses did not equal a courtesy, but venting his displeasure made him feel better.

The morning was blue and white and brilliant. Ice glazed the tree branches and the air sparkled like spun sugar. A fresh fall of snow blanketed the ground and made a satisfying crunch beneath Jonathan's feet as he ran.

After one mile, he'd stopped fuming about the party. After two, he had forgotten about last night.

He focused on his breathing, on the rhythmic swing of his arms and legs and the sting of the wind on his face, and as he turned toward home, he imagined he was an Olympic runner, out to capture the world record.

He picked up the pace until his heart was pumping twice its normal rate, and when he got his second wind he worked on technique, keeping to an easy lope, elbows close to his sides, inhaling deeply, exhaling slowly in long steamy breaths that curled behind him on the frosty air.

By the time he reached his apartment, the muscles in his legs were twitching with fatigue. His mouth felt as if it were lined with flannel and his ears and the tip of his nose were numb, but his mind was clear and he felt as if he had won a gold medal.

Certainly he had overcome his frustration at the minimal inroads he had made on his clients' accounts.

The price-earnings projection for one of the stocks he'd recommended came out ridiculously low, no matter how many times he checked his figures. He knew that someone had made a mistake, probably in data entry, but damned if he could find it.

His thoughts leaped ahead to the day's work, and he started the coffee maker on his way to the bathroom. After a hot, relaxing shower, shaved and dressed in faded cords and a V-necked sweater, he returned to the kitchen.

The calm lasted through his first cup of coffee. He was just pouring the second when he heard voices in the hall; feminine voices, shrill and giggly.

He growled an oath, and as the parade of visitors continued and the chandelier started to sway, he bundled a sheaf of computer printouts into his briefcase.

If he couldn't get any work done at home, he would transfer his base of operations to the office. But only for the remainder of the weekend.

He was not unreasonable. He enjoyed a party as much as the next man, but his tolerance had its limits. He would give Paulette what's-her-name till Monday to clean up her act. If she didn't, he'd have her tossed out of the studio so fast, her dizzy little head would still be spinning next Christmas.

HER LAST NAME WAS D'AMBOISE.

He learned that Monday morning, from the stencil she had taped to her mailbox.

When he got home that evening, she was waiting for him in the vestibule, surrounded by gift boxes, shopping bags and a scrawny Scotch pine.

"It's pathetic, I know," she said, straightening one of the branches on the tree. "The man at the Jaycee's lot was getting ready to burn it, and it looked so sad. I simply had to rescue it."

She smiled. Jonathan didn't.

Seen close up, she was even more attractive than he'd thought, with green eyes as beguiling as her smile and the sort of figure most men would weave fantasies around. But he was not most men, nor did he see anything amusing in a person ascribing human feelings to a Christmas tree. He studied Paulette impassively as he inquired, "How may I help you?"

"I wanted to apologize for the disturbance this weekend," she replied. "I promise you, my friends aren't always so rowdy. I guess you can chalk it up to the season. Anyway, a couple of the guys came down Friday night to invite you to join the party, but by then you'd gone out."

Jonathan turned away and reached into his overcoat pocket for his latchkey. "I was home," he said. "I just quit answering the door."

Paulette was taken aback. As a rule men responded to her with indulgence, sometimes with warmth, sometimes with fervor. She would rather make friends than enemies, but if her tall, distinguished neighbor wanted to be a grouch, that was okay with her.

There was one thing she wouldn't put up with, however, and that was being treated as if she were a nonentity. If Jonathan Day thought he could *dismiss* her, he had another think coming.

"I'm sorry to be a nuisance," she said brightly. "I tried to rouse the couple in Apartment Three—"

"They've gone to Milwaukee for the holidays."

"Oh. Well, Jack, the point is, I wouldn't bother you if I had any choice, but I'm afraid I'm locked out of my apartment."

Jonathan glanced at her over his shoulder, his face stony. Acquaintances called him Mr. Day, business associates J.D. His clients called him Jon. His mother and one or two lifelong friends called him Jonny, but no one called him Jack. *No one.*

"I know what you're thinking," Paulette continued, her voice bubbling with good cheer. "You're thinking I forgot my key, but I didn't."

"Where is it then?"

"Stuck in the dead bolt. I can't turn the key and I can't pull it out. I wondered if I might use your phone to call the superintendent."

"That's not necessary." Jonathan opened the door and bowed from the waist. "If you'd care to wait inside, I'll have a look at the dead bolt. It may be the lock just needs oiling, and if I can't fix it, I'll call a locksmith."

"What about the owner? Won't he object?"

"Not at all, Miss D'Amboise. You see, I'm the owner."

Jonathan stepped into his apartment and motioned Paulette to follow him. While he drew the blinds and turned on lamps, she stood just inside the living room, mulling over her discovery.

In her search for a sublet, she had dealt with RentFinders, a firm that supervised the leasing and maintenance for some of Madison's largest apartment complexes. But RentFinders also managed a few smaller buildings, like this converted Dutch Colonial gem in the University Heights district, most of them for absentee owners. Until now, she hadn't realized her landlord lived on the premises. She wasn't sure she liked the idea.

"Do you own a lot of rentals?" she asked.

"Just the four in this building," Jonathan replied with a brusque shake of his head.

"Then, if you don't mind my asking, why the secrecy? Why don't you save the commission and handle the apartments yourself?"

"That, Miss D'Amboise, would be a false economy. I can't afford to spend my time changing light bulbs and unclogging drains."

His tone was just short of insulting. A less hardy soul might have been put off, but if Paulette was discouraged she didn't let on.

She draped her coat over the back of a chair and herself across one end of the sofa. She was wearing a narrow dark skirt and a fuzzy green sweater that matched her eyes and tantalized Jonathan's imagination. As she snuggled deeper into the upholstery, her body seemed boneless and seductive.

"Confident, aren't you," she purred. "I like that in a man."

Jonathan was flattered in spite of himself, which forced him to admit that Paulette had a come-on that wouldn't quit. But he was not about to succumb to her allure. He escaped temptation by striding into the kitchen, but he could not escape her questions.

"Tell me, Jack," she called. "What do you do that makes your time so valuable?"

He opened the cupboard beneath the sink and found the spray can of WD40. "I'm a business consultant," he replied in simple terms even a redheaded dimwit should be able to understand. "I advise people how to invest their money."

"For fun and profit?"

The teasing lilt in Paulette's voice made him wonder if he had underestimated her intelligence. "Just for profit," he said. "My clients can worry about their own fun."

"You sound like a financial expert."

"And you, Miss D'Amboise, sound like an expert on fun."

"Shall I count the ways?"

"No," Jonathan replied, scowling. "I can figure them out for myself."

"Then you must agree that life's too short to take it seriously."

"On the contrary. I'd say just the opposite."

Paulette's laughter was soft and musical. "Shame on you, Jack. 'Tis the season to be jolly. Where's your Christmas spirit?"

"Bah, humbug," Jonathan retorted, and on that note he left the apartment.

It didn't take long to confirm that the studio's dead bolt was well and truly jammed. He gave the lock a squirt of oil and managed to retrieve Paulette's key, but the lock wouldn't turn. After several tries, he admitted the only thing left to do was to go back to his place and call a locksmith.

While he was on the phone in the kitchen, he was peripherally aware of Paulette prowling about the living room. He wondered what she was up to, and finally, overcome by curiosity, he took the phone into the dining alcove so that he could keep tabs on her.

As luck would have it, keeping an eye on Paulette was not an unpleasant task. She reminded him somehow of a butterfly, quick and bright and elusive. She moved as if she had wings on her feet, flitting here and there, pausing now and again to smooth her hand over a cushion or to glance through the photographs on the mantel. She stopped to admire the chess pieces on the coffee table, but even when she was perfectly still, she seemed to be poised for flight.

She picked up one of the rooks and weighed it in her palm, tracing its fluted ivory column with her fingertips. He was about to ask her to put it down when she returned the rook, carefully, to the proper square on the chessboard.

She looked toward the kitchen and intercepted his gaze. "Any luck?" she asked.

"I've reached an answering service," he replied. "I'm waiting for the operator to connect me."

She nodded and wandered to the far corner of the living room, studying the wall unit that housed the stereo and TV.

"Who's your opponent?" she asked.

"Pardon me?"

"The chess game. Who are you playing?"

"Sergei Zhenkov."

Her eyes widened with recognition, which wasn't surprising considering that Zhenkov was a star of stage, screen and ballet who had been making headlines ever since his defection from the Soviet Union.

"Is he a client?"

"Yes," said Jonathan. "He's also a friend."

He expected Paulette to ask a barrage of gossipy "What's he really like?" questions. Instead, she looked at her wristwatch and said, "My hands are gritty from the Christmas tree. Mind if I use your bathroom to wash up?"

Jonathan suspected the handwashing excuse was her passport to the rest of his apartment, but she disappeared into the hallway before he could suggest she use the kitchen sink.

"Help yourself," he muttered. But his sarcasm was wasted on her.

She opened the bathroom door and called, "Great tub, Jack! You could float the Bismarck in it. All I've got upstairs is a stall shower—but of course you know that."

When she turned on the taps, it occurred to him that she might be running the water to cover the sounds of her snooping, but in less than a minute she turned the water off. She sauntered back to the dining alcove just as the operator put him through to the locksmith, and while he described the problem with the dead bolt, Paulette sat in the swivel chair at the computer terminal and considered the decor.

The dining alcove had been furnished by IBM, and aside from a pine Shaker desk that reflected the Spartan elegance of its owner, the living room was tweedy and contemporary, remarkable only for its neatness.

All in all, her landlord's taste in furniture revealed nothing about him she didn't already know. A single look at Jonathan Day made it clear that he was sober, industrious, self-disciplined and responsible to a fault.

He was the kind of man who took vitamins and saw his tailor once a year, his dentist twice and his barber every other week; the kind whose conscience was clear, whose checkbook balanced, and whose future was indelibly mapped out. He was the kind of man all her women friends wanted to marry; the kind her best friend, Annie Leyland—now Gallagher—*had* married last Thanksgiving.

In short, he was the kind of man her parents introduced her to whenever she went home. Which brought up the question of why she found him intriguing.

She swung the chair around so that she could see Jonathan through the kitchen doorway, studying him openly while he concluded his phone call.

He was good-looking, all right. No doubt about that, even if he did seem squeaky clean, as if he had just been starched and drip-dried. And she had always had a weakness for square-jawed Lincolnesque men with blue eyes. That would account for casual curiosity, but it didn't explain the scope of her interest, which bypassed casual and went directly to— What?

A brief flirtation?

A spot of holiday romance?

Heaven help me, she thought. Annie's wedding must be getting to me. I'm not making any sense at all.

The last tiny spark of romance in her soul had perished the day she'd heard news of Cary Grant's death. How could she entertain the idea of having a fling with Jonathan Day? He was stern and disapproving, and not her type at all.

But he seemed deliciously shockable. Perhaps that was his attraction. Or maybe she just wanted to muss him up a little. And he had the biggest stereo speakers she'd ever seen, not to mention that glorious tub that reminded her of a Roman bath, with a Jacuzzi to boot!

Surely a Jack with those credentials couldn't be all work and no play.

"The locksmith will be here in half an hour," said Jonathan, hanging up the phone. "May I offer you a cup of coffee while you're waiting?"

"No, thanks. I have a dinner date at seven." Frowning slightly, Paulette swiveled toward the computer terminal. Half an hour didn't give her much time to soften Jonathan's opinion of her, but soften it she would.

She surveyed the keyboard and disk drive, the printer and mound of data sheets. Force of habit made her scan the printout at the top of the stack, and suddenly she smiled.

"Did you know you've misplaced a decimal?"

"Are you sure? Let me see that." Jonathan grabbed the printout and hastily read it, and there, near the center of the page, was the error he'd been looking for since Friday. "My God, I don't believe it! I've checked these figures a dozen times and never noticed that decimal. Then you come along and spot it right away."

"Well, Jack, it happens. People see what they expect to see."

Was she referring to the price-earnings ratio or to his attitude toward her? She gave him a barely perceptible wink, and in that moment it occurred to him that she might have hidden assets. While they waited for the locksmith, he tried to determine what they were.

He discovered that she worked at Shorewood College. "I'm the assistant registrar," she told him.

Shorewood was a privately endowed liberal arts college. It was small by comparison with the University of Wisconsin, but even so the registrar must process thousands of transcripts and applications for enrollment every semester. He supposed that explained Paulette's familiarity with printouts.

His gaze wandered from her coppery curls to her stylish, but impractical, high-heeled shoes.

She was smaller than he'd thought, maybe five-three without the heels. And fine-boned. Petite. Standing close to her, he felt acutely aware of her femininity.

"Funny," he said, half to himself, "you don't look like a data processor."

"Thank you, Jack. I take that as a compliment."

He realized he was staring at her breasts, and shifted his attention to her legs. "Am I to assume you're not a fan of computers?"

Paulette lifted a delicate red-gold eyebrow. "Does a dog have fleas?"

Jonathan had no trouble interpreting this as an affirmative response, but he was still trying to decide whether it was also an insult when the locksmith arrived.

His next discovery came when the dead bolt had been replaced and the man from Roy's Key Service was totaling his bill. "I think you're gonna be happy with that new dead bolt," he said.

"I'm sure I will be," Jonathan replied.

"We're running a special on 'em this month," said the locksmith, scribbling on his order pad. "It's only gonna cost you twenty-two fifty, plus the eighteen-buck trip charge and seventy cents apiece for the keys. Add five percent for the governor, and you got a bargain at forty-four dollars."

Paulette cleared her throat. "I believe you've shorted yourself a dollar."

Jonathan glanced up from his checkbook, and the locksmith added the charges again.

"You're right, by golly!" he declared, beaming at Paulette.

She has a mind like an adding machine, Jonathan thought as he wrote out the check. *Does that mean she's calculating?*

To point out the error was honest; to point out the exact amount of the discrepancy seemed ostentatious, and he acknowledged that her facility with numbers might have struck him more favorably if she had been less of a show-off.

When the locksmith left, Jonathan offered to carry Paulette's packages upstairs. It seemed the gentlemanly thing to do. Besides, he couldn't wait to get a look at the studio and find out how much damage the party had done.

He followed her up the stairs, towing the Scotch pine. The tree left a thick trail of needles on the carpet, and he hoisted it over one shoulder to spare the janitor. When Paulette opened the studio door, he peered through the pine boughs, prepared for the worst.

The room was dark except for the swath of light from the hall, and he reached for the light switch. He flipped it on, but nothing happened.

"Are you having trouble with the electricity too?" he asked.

"Not that I know of."

Paulette's voice came from the direction of the kitchen. He heard a scratching sound as she struck a match. She lighted two candles, one on the counter, another on the range top, and as a wavering glow crept toward him, Jonathan realized how empty the studio was.

"I see you haven't finished moving in yet," he observed.

"Yes, I have."

"But you don't have any lamps," he said, and then, chiding himself for stating the obvious, "You don't have any furniture either."

"Not unless you count the lawn chairs," said Paulette. "No dishes, no glasses, no pots or pans—"

"No stereo," he said. "But I heard music the other night."

"One of my guests brought a boom box." The match burned her fingers, and she shook it out, muttering, "Darn it. I forgot to buy coat hangers again."

"I have extras you can use."

Paulette struck another match and rewarded him with a smile. "It's nice of you to offer, but I'll manage. You see, I don't have many clothes."

She knelt between the chairs and lighted a third candle, and as this circle of light seeped into the gloom he spotted the webbed nylon chaise she had shoved beneath the windows, a pillow and folded bedding at one end. This time she answered his question before he could ask it.

"That's where I sleep," she said, following her trail of candles into the bathroom.

Jonathan stared after her, astonished. Why would a woman squander her money on a molting Scotch pine and an assortment of Christmas ornaments when she didn't have a stick of indoor furniture? She didn't even own an alarm clock, for God's sake!

He couldn't decide whether she was a harmless flake or a femme fatale. Was she on the lam? Was she running away from something or someone? Would she skip out on next month's rent?

He envisioned all sorts of difficulties, and wanted to ask some probing questions so that he'd have a better idea what he was dealing with, but Paulette didn't give him the chance.

She had turned on the shower, and above the rushing water she called, "Thanks for your help, Jack. I'd invite you to stay a while, but I have to get ready for my date."

"Uh, yes. See you later," he shouted. His questions would have to keep. All except one. "Where do you want the tree?"

"Just put it down anywhere. And, Jack, be a dear, would you, and close the door on your way out."

Chapter Two

Thirty minutes later she returned to his apartment, wearing an expensive new dress. At least, the gauzy, teal-blue creation looked expensive to him. And Paulette looked stunning in it. She did a pirouette, and the soft floaty fabric whispered against her legs.

"I bought this especially for tonight." She smoothed a hand over one hip, adjusting the folds of the skirt. "You like?"

"Who wouldn't?"

Jonathan stared at her, bemused. He'd have sworn her eyes were green, yet now they were as blue as her dress.

"You're very observant," Paulette said when he commented on the change. "Some of my closest friends have never noticed my contacts, even though there have been times when I've gotten the lenses mixed up and gone around all day with one green eye and one blue one."

"Maybe your friends didn't want to embarrass you by pointing out the mistake."

"Maybe," Paulette replied, but her expression said she was skeptical.

"What's your natural eye color?"

"Does it matter?"

Jonathan supposed it didn't. Green, blue or polka-dotted, the color of Paulette's eyes made no difference to him. But still, he felt disappointed that she found it necessary to resort to artifice. He looked at her steadily, trying to detect which of her other charms might be illusions and which, if any, were genuine.

"The rest of me is real, Jack. Cross my heart. What you see is what you get."

His gaze automatically went to her bright, glossy hair.

"Want to check my roots?" she inquired.

"Do you want me to?"

His husky drawl made the suggestion seem indecent, and when he closed the door to the vestibule, Paulette opened it again.

"Ben'll be here any minute," she said. "I wouldn't want to miss him."

"Ben's your date?"

"I guess you could call him that. Anyway, I wondered if you happen to have any vanilla."

"Vanilla? Yes, I think so." Visibly puzzled, Jonathan led the way into the kitchen and pointed out the spice cabinet. "Help yourself," he said, wondering what she was concocting.

It soon became apparent that she was not making eggnog. When she found the vanilla, she dabbed the extract behind her ears, on the inside of her wrists, the crook of her elbows and the creamy pulse points at the base of her throat.

As she replaced the cap on the bottle, she noticed Jonathan watching her every move, his brows drawn in consternation. Smiling, she said, "I forgot to buy perfume, and I feel naked without it."

She held her wrist to her nose and sniffed once or twice, then extended her wrist to him.

"What do you think?"

Against his better judgment, Jonathan bent over her wrist, cradling it with his hand. Her skin was silky and cameo-fair, so translucent that he could trace the network of fine blue veins that threaded into her palm.

She smelled good enough to eat; good enough to kiss. Her fragrance made him think of sugar cookies; her smile of seduction. She was a provocative blend of guile and naïveté, an accomplished flirt who made him feel protective. He had an insane desire to take her in his arms—and quickly squelched it.

"You'll do," he said, and he moved away from her just as the street door opened, admitting a blast of wintry air and a blond giant of a man whom Paulette introduced as Ben Gallagher.

Ben greeted Paulette with a bear hug and Jonathan with a handshake. He was easygoing and personable. Under different circumstances, Jonathan might have responded amiably. But Ben was wearing a wedding ring, which forced Jonathan to lower his assessment of Paulette's standards by yet another notch.

If she was a home wrecker as well as a hedonist, she might be hiding out in the studio so that she wouldn't be named as corespondent in a divorce action, and if that were the case, he would be well advised to keep his distance. The last thing he needed was to get involved in a protracted court hearing.

"Ready to go, cupcake?" said Ben.

"I just have to get my coat," Paulette replied.

"I believe you left it in the living room," Jonathan said.

In the minute it took to find her coat, his imagination ran amok. He pictured Paulette and Gallagher locked in a passionate embrace. He pictured banner headlines proclaiming the studio a love nest. He pictured himself on the witness stand, being grilled by the plaintiff's attorney. "Did you, Jonathan Day, permit the defendant to meet his paramour in your apartment? Were you not in fact an accomplice to their deceit?"

He watched Gallagher take Paulette's arm and usher her through the vestibule, but in his mind's eye he saw a wronged wife, grieving children, outraged friends—

"'Night, Jack," Paulette called.

"Nice meeting you," said Ben.

The street door closed behind them, and a few seconds later Jonathan heard Gallagher start his car. He breathed a sigh of relief as the sound of the engine faded into the night.

"Thank God," he muttered. He'd thought they'd never leave. Now maybe he could get some work done.

His apartment was quiet. Too quiet.

As he had told Paulette, the couple in Number Three had gone to Milwaukee, and the students in Four, just across the hall, had also gone home for the holidays. For the time being he had the building to himself, but instead of enjoying the calm, making the most of it, he paced from room to room, thinking about Paulette, remembering the warmth of her smile, the eagerness with which she had awaited Ben Gallagher—and the innocence.

At quarter-hour intervals, he heard her phone ringing. The third time it rang, he decided she must have a lot of friends calling to say "Merry Christmas." Either that or one special friend who was desperate to reach her.

He had warmed-over spaghetti for supper, and afterward he poured himself a beer and tried to settle down with a prospectus for a convention center one of his clients had asked him to look into. He read the opening paragraph several times before he realized none of the information had registered, and at last he put the prospectus aside and resumed his restless pacing.

What if he had misjudged Paulette? What if Gallagher had no intention of leaving his wife? What if Paulette was only the latest in a series of infidelities? Wouldn't that make her as much a victim as the hapless Mrs. Gallagher?

And if Paulette was a victim, should he, Jonathan, make some sort of effort to save her from herself?

At ten o'clock Jonathan pulled on his sweats and went out for a run, but concern for Paulette dogged his heels every step of the way. When he got home, he showered and fell into bed, exhausted. But he didn't fall asleep until he heard Paulette come in, shortly after midnight.

JONATHAN WOULD HAVE BEEN more worried if he'd known that Paulette spent a good part of the evening thinking about him.

While he was pacing and brooding, she was ten miles away, at the Mariners Inn, proposing a toast to Anne and Ben Gallagher's future happiness. And while he ate leftover spaghetti, she ordered scampi and tried to uphold her end of the conversation by inquiring about her friends' wedding trip. But even then, Jonathan was not far from her thoughts.

"Hawaii was lovely," Anne replied. "You wouldn't believe the flowers."

"How was the weather?" Paulette asked.

"Sunny and mild," said Anne.

"You didn't get much of a tan."

The old Anne Leyland would have been flustered by Paulette's teasing, but the new Mrs. Gallagher didn't turn a hair. "We didn't get out much," she said.

"Someday we'll have to go back and see Waikiki," said Ben.

The melting glance the newlyweds exchanged made Paulette feel as if she'd wandered into a scene from an old romantic comedy, and as the meal progressed the feeling grew.

The Gallaghers held hands beneath the table. They kissed once or twice, but even when they weren't touching, it was obvious they were a closed corporation. They finished each other's sentences, laughed at the same jokes, and radiated a closeness Paulette envied. They ate whatever the waitress put in front of them, but Paulette doubted they tasted any of it.

And if she was a bit preoccupied, they were just too much in love to notice.

They were finishing their cheesecake before Anne got around to asking what Paulette had been up to the last few weeks. "Any promising men on your horizon?" Anne inquired.

"Not unless you count Alan Pierson," said Paulette.

"The new basketball coach at Shorewood?"

"That's the one. We're supposed to have dinner tomorrow night after the game with Whitewater, but that's the first date I've had in ages. I haven't had much of a social life lately." After a brief silence, Paulette added, "I guess you heard about the fire."

"Yes, of course," Anne replied, stricken. "I should have asked about it sooner."

"Hey, Annie, I understand. You've been busy with other things."

"But it must've been awful for you."

Paulette shuddered, recalling the explosion that had rocked the predawn stillness, the voracious flames and dense clouds of smoke. "It was quite an experience," she admitted. "The fire started with a buildup of methane from the landfill across the street, and once it got going those condominiums went up like a torch."

"My brother told us it happened the Friday after the wedding," said Ben.

"That's right," said Paulette.

"Was anyone hurt?"

"Not seriously, thank God. One of the firemen was overcome by fumes. He was admitted to the hospital and released the next day. And the woman next door was treated in the emergency room for minor burns. All things considered, though, it could've been much worse."

"According to Clint, you lost everything," Anne said.

"Just about." With a rueful shake of her head, Paulette said, "Ben, I can't tell you how grateful I am to your brother and his family. Clint insisted that I stay with them till I found an apartment, and his wife let me use her car to look for a place. Your nieces loaned me clothes, and when I found my sublet, your nephews threw a surprise party to make me feel at home."

"So Clint wasn't exaggerating," Anne murmured. "You really did lose everything."

"Everything but the lawn furniture, my address book, and the nightie I was wearing when the balloon went up. I even lost the gifts I'd bought for Christmas."

"Were you insured?" asked Ben.

Paulette grinned. "Does Santa have whiskers?"

"Well, how're you fixed for ready cash?"

"I'm fine, Ben. Honestly. My homeowner's policy provides a monthly housing stipend till the claim is settled, and it's more than adequate. It covers the rent, with enough left over for me to start replacing my wardrobe."

"What about Jack? Doesn't he pay his share?"

Anne's fork skidded across her plate, sending a sliver of cheesecake onto the tablecloth. "Who's Jack?" she demanded, turning to Paulette. "Have you been holding out on me?"

Paulette shook her head. She stared at Ben, uncomprehending. "Why should Jack pay my rent? I hardly know the man."

"Aren't you living together?" asked Ben.

"Heavens no! He's my landlord, that's all. He has the apartment downstairs, I have the studio upstairs, and if I have anything to say about it, never the twain shall meet."

"No foolin'?" said Ben.

"No foolin' around either," Paulette declared.

Anne smiled and propped her chin in her hand, and glancing from Anne to Ben, Paulette recognized that neither of them believed her.

"It's true," she cried. Her voice carried across the hushed intimacy of the restaurant, and the men at the adjoining table turned to ogle her. "I never met Jonathan Day till this evening, but I can tell you we have nothing in common but our address. He's into computers and statistics and chess. He uses a different side of his *brain* than I do. He calls me 'Miss D'Amboise.' He doesn't even *like* me—"

"Whoa, Paulette, I'm convinced," said Ben. After a conspiratorial glance at his wife, he added, "I just have one question. If Jack's only interest in you is business, why did he object to your going out with me?"

"And why," said Anne, "are you blushing?"

Why, indeed?

It was completely out of character for her to lose her cool, yet she was blushing like a schoolgirl.

And why couldn't she get Jonathan out of her mind? Was it possible her interest in him was more than superficial?

The rest of the evening passed in a blur. It seemed essential to Paulette that she resolve these issues, but an hour after the Gallaghers dropped her at her apartment, she hadn't come up with the answers. All she had was more questions.

She put on her nightgown and her new quilted robe. She removed her contacts and washed her face. She made up her bed on the chaise, but she couldn't get to sleep. After tossing and turning for another hour, she decided a snack might help her relax.

She lighted the candles and went into the kitchen, where she assembled the ingredients for fluffer-nutters, a sinfully rich confection made of graham crackers topped with crunchy peanut butter, marshmallow fluff, chocolate chips and caramel morsels. She popped the crackers under the broiler for a minute, and voilà! She had a gooey, indigestible treat worth staying awake for.

Curled up in one of the lawn chairs, surrounded by shadows, she ate a bite of fluffer-nutter and sipped instant coffee and wondered where she'd gotten the idea that an unfurnished studio would be less depressing than a motel room.

Of course, the studio was only temporary. The sublet expired at the end of March, and her insurance claim on the condo should be settled in the next month or so. In the meantime, if she couldn't live without furniture for this place, nothing was stopping her from buying some.

Except common sense.

It seemed practical to wait till she'd bought another condo before she burdened herself with sofas and bureaus and major appliances. After all, why move everything twice? But a TV set or a radio would not be out of line. If she had a radio right now she could tune in one of the late-night deejays to fill the silence and help her make it through the night.

She reached for another fluffer-nutter, wishing she had a book...a magazine...even a newspaper. If she had remembered to start her subscription to the *Wisconsin State Journal*, she could check the classifieds and see what sort of condos were on the market, maybe even find one or two prospects to look at tomorrow.

"No, today," she murmured, correcting herself. "It's later than you think."

Both literally and figuratively.

On April 1 she would be *thirty*. God, it seemed unreal! Turning thirty was something that happened to other people, not to her. Where had her twenties gone?

She washed down a bite of fluffer-nutter with coffee as black as her mood, and lifted the telephone onto her lap. She had started to dial Anne's old number before she recalled that Annie didn't live there anymore. What's more, Anne had a husband to consider, and from the yearning way she had looked at Ben all evening, she might not welcome a phone call.

After a momentary hesitation, Paulette replaced the receiver and helped herself to another cracker.

She hadn't thought of herself as being hooked on materialism until the fire destroyed almost everything she owned, and until tonight, she hadn't recognized how much she depended on Anne's advice, on her refusal to pass judgment and on her unflagging optimism.

Paulette wasn't foolish enough to think marriage would change Anne's disposition, but it was bound to make subtle differences in their friendship. Such changes, she realized, were inevitable. But that didn't make them any more palatable.

Sighing, Paulette set her coffee cup on the floor, then rose and went into the bathroom, where she confronted her image in the mirror.

By candlelight, without cosmetics and without her contacts, she didn't look a day over twenty-five, but she was not reassured. "You're losing it," she told herself, and although she wasn't sure what "it" was, she knew this was true.

Her features seemed soft and defenseless, and she turned her back on the mirror, annoyed with her uncertainty.

She needed someone to talk to. Someone understanding. Someone wise. Someone who would sympathize and tell her everything was going to be all right. But just now she would settle for hearing another human voice.

She hurried to the guest closet and located her address book. Her steps were purposeful as she returned to her chair by the phone.

On most any other night, she would have phoned her sister, but Nicole was in the throes of her second divorce. She had her own troubles and Paulette didn't want to add to them.

Her parents were out, too. Her father was better at preaching than listening, and her mother's idea of moral support was to point out Paulette's shortcomings. But she had dozens of friends, pages and pages of them, all listed neatly in her little black book.

Paulette smiled as she opened the book, but her smile vanished as she skimmed the names in the *AB* section and found no one she cared to confide in. She rushed through the *C*'s and *D*'s, pausing only to read the personal comments she had attached to an occasional entry; reminders that Gary Carr was a "good dancer," and Sean Dennison looked "terrific in a dinner jacket."

She was midway through the alphabet when she came upon Richard Lowery's name, and for the first time she hesitated.

Richard and she had dated for several months, until he'd asked her to marry him. Then their romance, like most of her flirtations, had died of attrition; unconsummated, unsung and for the most part unmourned.

She was still fond of Richard though; fond enough that she was tempted to give him a call and suggest they get together for a drink, maybe reminisce about the pleasant times they had shared.

But, she reminded herself, Richard wasn't satisfied with fondness, and she could not envision herself married to him.

She pictured herself at seventy, seeing Richard's face next to hers on the pillow when she woke up in the morning. She pictured him gaunt and graying, with liver spots on his forehead and tufts of hair growing out of his ears. Even when she imagined herself with failing vision, it was not a pretty sight.

She shivered and flipped to the next section, bypassing Alan Pierson's name without a second glance. By the time she reached the *QRS*'s, she had given up hope of finding anyone she wanted to call, and as she closed the book she asked herself, "With five rooms of belongings to choose from, what kind of person saves her address book from a fire?"

She didn't like the answer.

As she bit into the last cracker, Paulette acknowledged that she felt no particular attachment for any of the men she'd listed in the book. She had gone out with most of them because they were safe, because they hadn't expected love or marriage or any sort of intimacy. All they'd asked of her was that she decorate their lives for a while. And they were transient. She had written their names in pencil. If she were to erase them, they would leave no more trace in her life than their expunged names would leave on the paper.

"The same could be said of me," she murmured.

With the possible exception of her parents, her sister, and perhaps Anne, she had touched no one's life.

It suddenly seemed imperative that she rectify this situation, but she wasn't sure how to go about it or where to begin.

She leaned back in the chair and stared at the ceiling while she grappled with this predicament. After a few minutes, the address book slipped off her lap and fell to the floor, unnoticed. Her eyelids were so heavy, she could scarcely keep them open, and she realized it must be very late.

The studio was chilly, the crackers were gone and her coffee was cold, but the scent of the Scotch pine gave a pungent cheerfulness to the room and provided just the inspiration she needed.

"I'll start tonight," she decided. "With Jonathan Day."

She could make a project of him, bring a bit of Christmas cheer into his life, show him how to enjoy himself, get him to loosen up and have a good time....

She imagined Jonathan's clear blue eyes brightened by a smile, and her mouth turned up at the corners. She imagined waking in the morning to see his face next to hers on the pillow, and her heart skipped a beat.

As she carried her plate and cup to the waste can in the kitchen, it occurred to her that if her project succeeded, Jonathan might be more than she could handle. But she wouldn't let herself reconsider.

"It's either Jack or overdosing on fluffer-nutters," she told herself.

She really had no alternative.

Chapter Three

On Tuesday morning Paulette canceled her date with the basketball coach. That evening when Jonathan got home from work, she was waiting outside his door with yet another Christmas tree. His jaw dropped when he saw the enormous blue spruce.

"Isn't it a beauty?" she asked.

He nodded, eyeing the tree. It scraped the ceiling and took up most of the floor space in the vestibule. He had to walk sideways to get around it.

"How did you get it through the door?"

"The cabdriver gave me a hand," said Paulette, "but it wasn't easy."

Jonathan believed her. The tree must be heavy. The bottom of the trunk had a five-inch diameter.

He opened his door and tossed his topcoat and briefcase inside, resigned to the task ahead. Getting the spruce upstairs was going to be a hell of a job, but the sooner he got started, the sooner he'd be able to get back to work. He took off his sport jacket and began rolling up his sleeves without bothering to ask whether Paulette wanted his help with the tree. There was no way she could manage it by herself.

"What happened to the pine?" he asked.

"I decorated it."

"But I thought—didn't you throw it out?"

"Why would I do that? Oh, I'll admit it looked pretty scruffy last night, but you'd be surprised at the difference some ornaments and a few miles of tinsel made."

"I'm sure it's festive, but what are you going to do with two trees?" The moment the question was out, Jonathan threw up one hand to forestall her answer. "Wait. Don't tell me. Let me guess. You're running a clandestine Christmas tree lot in the studio."

"Would my lease permit that?"

"Only if you cut your landlord in for ten percent of the gross."

"Forget it then, and guess again."

"You're making your own paper."

"No, not this year. Maybe next."

"You're establishing a home for wayward squirrels."

Paulette shook her head, green eyes shining with merriment. "Sorry, Jack, you're not even close."

"I give up." Jonathan made one last fold in his shirt sleeve and hefted the butt end of the tree. It was heavier than it looked, even when Paulette lifted the crown. "So tell me, where do you want this one?"

"I thought maybe the window bay."

He gave the tree a quarter turn, angling it toward the stairway. Then her answer sank in and he stopped, one foot hovering above the bottom step.

"Just a minute," he said. "The studio doesn't have bay windows."

"No, but your living room does."

"My living room? Are you saying you bought this tree for me?"

"Bingo! I couldn't help noticing that you don't have any decorations—"

"You're much too generous," Jonathan broke in stiffly.

"Don't be silly, Jack. I'm just trying to be a good neighbor."

"And I appreciate the effort, but I can't accept the tree."

He sounded less than thrilled and he looked downright grumpy. The way he was glaring at her made Paulette wonder if her time might be better spent whipping up a double batch of fluffer-nutters.

"Don't you like blue spruce?" she said. "Maybe I should've bought you a pine."

"You shouldn't have bought me anything. You need too many things yourself."

"But Jack, the point is I did buy it, and I can't take it back. There was a sign at the lot that said All Sales Final."

"Then will you let me reimburse you for it?"

"I wouldn't dream of it, but if it's the expense that's bothering you—" Paulette saw by Jonathan's expression that she had struck a nerve, and she hastened to explain. "Appearances to the contrary, I am not hard-pressed for cash."

She told him about the fire and her allowance and the insurance settlement she was expecting, and at last, because it seemed to mean so much to her, Jonathan said, "All right, Paulette, I'll take the tree. But I don't have any ornaments, and if I did, I don't know when I'd find time to decorate it. I have two days' worth of work to finish tonight."

"Don't worry, Jack. I'll take care of the decorations."

His acceptance was grudging at best, but so what? She chose to look at the bright side, and she was encouraged by his use of her first name.

We're making progress, she thought as they wrestled the spruce through the doorway and into his living room, and when Jonathan had jockeyed the tree to a spot near the windows and positioned it on its stand, she favored him with a smile guaranteed to melt the coldest heart.

"There now. Isn't that gorgeous?"

Jonathan didn't answer. He took a deep breath and held it while he counted to ten. Twice.

Paulette saw his lips move. She knew that his forbearance was dangerously near the breaking point and shooed him toward his computer.

"Go about your business," she said. "Pretend I'm not here. I'll be quiet as a mouse, you'll see. You won't even know I'm around."

"That's a laugh," Jonathan muttered. "You couldn't be inconspicuous if you tried; not if you were caught in a blackout at the bottom of a mine shaft."

"Can I help it if I attract attention? It's part of my nature."

"Part of your charm?"

Paulette shrugged. "You'll have to decide that for yourself. All I can tell you is, some people are born with an aptitude for math or languages. Some are born with a talent for music. As it happens, I was born with a flair for drama—"

"You're flamboyant," Jonathan said, "and you make the most of it. I'm amazed you'll bother playing to an audience of one. You need to be noticed as much as you need air to breathe or water to drink."

For the second time in as many days, Paulette felt herself blushing. "Thank you, Dr. Day, for that pearl of instant wisdom."

Jonathan's smile was more mocking than amused. "C'mon, Paulette, tell the truth. You love being the center of attention. You thrive on it."

Her face felt hot, so she dropped to her knees and began picking up the needles that had fallen from the spruce to conceal her rising color from Jonathan.

It wasn't as if he'd told her anything new about herself. When she was only six, she had interrupted a moment of silent prayer with an impromptu chorus of "Da Doo Ron Ron." After church that day, her father had told her, "In the future, if you must sing a solo, please make your selection from the hymnal."

Her mother, ever the disciplinarian, had grounded her for a week and given her a lecture. "Your father's too easy on you, Paulette. For the next seven days, I want you to give sober reflection to the way you disrupted this morning's services. Someone has to teach you that you cannot go through life being the bride at every wedding and the corpse at every funeral."

The macabre turn of that suggestion triggered its share of nightmares, but her parents' reaction taught Paulette one lesson: If she got into mischief, her mother and father would sit up and take notice.

So she hadn't mended her ways.

Even now there were times she went to incredible lengths to occupy the spotlight, but she preferred to give the impression of spontaneity, especially when her behavior was staged. And she resented the ease with which Jonathan saw through her.

He made her sound spoiled and scheming, as if she were still a recalcitrant six-year-old. He made her feel exposed, vulnerable— One of the spruce needles punctured the skin of her palm. She started and gave a muted yelp as blood welled into the scratch.

"I'll get the Band-Aids," said Jonathan, starting toward the bathroom.

"Don't bother. It's nothing."

He did an about-face. "I'll get the vacuum cleaner, then. You'll never get all that debris without it."

She sat on her heels, dabbing at the scratch with a Kleenex, while he dragged the cleaner out of the pantry and began running it over the carpet. When the bleeding stopped, she got to her feet and returned to the vestibule for the things she had bought to decorate the tree.

She'd trimmed the pine in pink and silver, with white lace rosettes and a dainty porcelain angel for the top. But the spruce required a masculine theme.

Taking her cue from Jonathan's living room, she had planned to keep it simple and homespun, and had supplied herself with cranberries and popcorn for stringing, lengths of red velvet ribbon to tie on the branches, some crocheted snowflakes and two dozen small brass hunting horns.

The tree looked bigger than it had on the lot. So big it was somewhat daunting. As she settled in the living room with needle and thread, preparing to string the cranberry-popcorn garland, she realized she had her work cut out. And not just with trimming the tree. Winning Jonathan's cooperation was going to be an uphill battle.

He had barricaded himself at his computer behind a stack of data sheets, and for the next forty-five minutes he seemed absorbed by his printouts, except for an occasional stroll to the living room to raid the popcorn.

His first foray prompted Paulette to work faster. His third made her want to slap his hand. On his fifth approach, she frowned and bit her lip, forcing back a protest. Her scowl faded when she saw a glint of laughter in his eyes.

She kept her vow of silence while he poured the last handful of popcorn from the sack and retraced his path to the dining alcove, grinning all the way.

"Cat got your tongue, Paulette?"

She crumpled the empty bag and hurled it at him. "No," she answered sweetly, "but some dirty rat stole my popcorn."

Still grinning, Jonathan wadded the sack tighter and threw it back to her. "I was only trying to help."

"By eating the decorations? How considerate."

He raised one hand, fingers folded in the Boy Scout salute. "Would I lie to you?"

She replied with a hand signal of a different sort, and began collecting her supplies.

"Temper, temper," he cautioned.

She leaped to her feet and confronted him, hands on her hips. "If you want me to leave, say so. Don't play these childish games."

"You're the one who's being childish, Paulette. Just because I ate your popcorn, that's no reason to pick up your cranberries and go home. Can't you take a joke?"

"Of course I can, but I'm not in the habit of joking about tradition."

"Tradition?" he repeated, shaking his head. "Does that mean you descend on some unsuspecting stranger every Christmas?"

"You're the first," Paulette answered hotly, "and you'll probably be the last."

She scooped up her shopping bag and headed for the door, but with two long strides Jonathan cut in front of her, blocking the way.

"What makes you think I want you to leave? All I'm saying is, it'd take a week to string enough popcorn for that tree."

Paulette drew herself to her full height and shifted the shopping bag to both arms, holding it between them like a shield. "I suppose you have a better idea?"

"As a matter of fact, I do." He reached for the parcel, but her grip on it tightened. "If you want to hang food on the tree, I'd suggest we stick to candy canes."

We. He'd actually said *we*. Was this the first sign of involvement? She raised hopeful eyes to his. "I'm willing to compromise if you are," she said, "but I don't have any candy canes."

"That's easily remedied. We'll go out and buy some."

Jonathan reached for the parcel again, and this time she let him take it. "I'll get my coat," she said, before he could change his mind.

She left him rummaging through the bag, and she was halfway to the studio when he called, "You don't have any lights."

She leaned over the banister and replied, "I wasn't sure you'd want them."

"As long as we're at it, we might as well get some."

Had Jonathan decided the quickest way to get rid of her was to help trim the tree? Was he humoring her?

Could be, Paulette thought, but that was all the encouragement she needed. For now.

She broke into a smile and took the remaining stairs two at a time.

Chapter Four

From the first time she saw Jonathan, Paulette had operated on the assumption that beneath his conservative banker's-gray suit beat a conservative banker's heart.

In the twenty-four hours since they'd met, he had been aloof and businesslike. He had kept a dignified distance and tried to wither her with a stare. He had displayed flashes of wit and one or two disturbing insights, but she saw no reason to change her opinion of him until he climbed behind the wheel of his car.

The car was a revelation in itself; low slung, sporty and fire-engine red, with the kind of chassis engineers called state-of-the-art. She thought it resembled a beetle on steroids that someone had squashed, but it most emphatically was not a banker's car.

"What do you think?" Jonathan asked, giving the instrument panel an affectionate pat.

"Nice," Paulette replied. She fastened her seat belt and realized Jonathan was waiting for her to say something more. "*Very* nice."

That seemed to satisfy him.

"I keep this baby in racing tune," he said. "She may not be new, but wait till you see her perform."

Paulette knew almost nothing about cars. She didn't recognize the make or model, but she didn't have to be an expert to know that Jonathan drove like a fiend.

From the instant he revved the engine and pulled away from the curb until he careened into the parking lot at the nearest mall, she clung to the edge of her seat, her teeth clamped tight to keep from screaming, and wondered where all the traffic cops were when she needed one.

They sped through the lanes of parked cars in a series of heart-stopping one-eighties, and as they skidded into an empty slot she promised herself, if she was lucky enough to survive the G-forces on the ride home, she would never again, under any circumstances, set foot in Jonathan's car.

The discount store was mobbed and overheated. In the center aisle, customers circled the clearance tables like sharks in a feeding frenzy. The cash registers played touch-tone jingles. A few aisles away in records and tapes, Elvis was singing "Blue Christmas," and from somewhere at the back of the store, a child was shrieking for its mommy.

Just inside the swinging doors, Jonathan hauled her to a stop. "I just remembered why I try to avoid shopping this time of year."

Paulette linked arms with him, and together they plunged into the throng.

Another surprise awaited her in the decorations department. Considering the crowd, her inclination was to choose the brand with either the lowest price or the biggest markdown and make a run for the checkout counter, but Jonathan refused to be stampeded.

He made it clear he would not be satisfied until he had read the fine print on the cartons and compared unit prices.

Paulette was fascinated by his transformation from reckless driver to careful shopper, and more than a little miffed that she had given up supper with Alan Pierson to spend the evening with a man who found bargain hunting more noteworthy than he found her.

Jonathan was punching numbers into his pocket calculator when it occurred to her that he might bring the same thoroughness to everything he did. Was he always so single-minded and intense? she wondered. In bed, for instance?

The recurring idea of Jonathan as a lover was so disconcerting that her step faltered. She stumbled into him, bumping his elbow and knocking the calculator to the floor. It shattered on impact, and shards of plastic flew in every direction. She watched him bend down to pick up the mangled pieces of circuitry and casing, too stunned to offer an apology.

"C-can you fix it?" she stammered.

Jonathan didn't reply. He didn't have to. The answer was spread the length and width of the aisle. He was startled by Paulette's clumsiness, and amazed that she had asked such a question.

She took a deep breath and seemed to emerge from her daze. "Well, Jack," she said with a shaky little laugh, "I guess that's one of the hazards of shopping so close to Christmas."

Jonathan straightened. He gave her a long, searching look, and then he smiled. "You may be right," he said. "In which case, I'd suggest we get out of here before one of us gets hurt."

JUST OUTSIDE THE MALL, Paulette paused to button her coat. Jonathan pulled on his gloves, shifted his shopping bag to his left hand, and took a firm grip on her elbow.

His touch warmed her. His palm was broad and powerful, and despite his fleece-lined gloves and the down insulation of her sleeve, she sensed a degree of possessiveness in his grasp.

Her arm tingled. A frisson of awareness zigzagged along her spine. She stole a glance at him as they set off across the parking lot, and nearly lost her footing on a patch of ice.

Jonathan hugged her arm to his side and said, "This blacktop's like a skating rink. Watch your step."

Good advice, thought Paulette. If she insisted on seeing Jonathan Day, it was vital that she keep her wits about her. If she didn't watch her step, only God knew what might happen.

They arrived at Jonathan's car and he unlocked the passenger door. He waited till she was seated, then bent down to wedge the shopping bag into the space next to her feet.

"Are you in a hurry to get home?" he asked.

She shoved her hands into her coat pockets, repressing the urge to brush back the shock of hair that had fallen over his forehead. "Why?" she replied warily. "What did you have in mind?"

"A steak. Maybe some seafood."

"How can you think of dinner after all that popcorn?"

"The popcorn was an appetizer. Now I'm ready for the main course."

He also wanted answers to a few questions.

Paulette's explanation about the fire had resolved his concern that she would trash the studio or try to defraud him, but he was worried about her affair with Ben Gallagher, and this seemed the perfect opportunity to ease his conscience. He would take her to a restaurant and ply her with food and drink. He'd flatter her, pay her compliments, turn on the charm. And when he had won her confidence, he would talk to her like a Dutch uncle.

Only he didn't feel avuncular right now. Not when she was almost in his arms.

He leaned closer, and she exhaled on a sigh. Her breath caressed his cheek. His hand abandoned the frozen crispness of the shopping bag and moved slowly toward her knee. Her soft pink mouth was mere inches away from his mouth, and his fingers were about to claim their prize when a pickup rattled to a stop directly behind his car.

"Hey, buddy, you coming or going?"

"Going," Jonathan answered reluctantly, pushing himself erect. He circled the rear of his car and got behind the wheel. His hand shook as he fitted the key into the ignition. He attributed it to the cold.

"How about it, Paulette? Shall we stop for a bite to eat?"

"I had a late lunch," she said. "I'm not very hungry."

"You can keep me company, though. Order a salad or something."

Jonathan's smile was earnest and engaging, and when she thought it over, it seemed safer not to be alone with him. At least for the time being. Besides, as he gunned the motor and sped away from the mall, she remembered how much she dreaded the drive home.

"All right, Jack. You talked me into it."

She hoped he would stop at a restaurant en route to his apartment. Instead he took her for a hair-raising ride over winding back roads, to an out-of-the-way supper club on the edge of town.

"Looks like we'll have plenty of privacy here," Jonathan remarked.

Aside from a few cars huddled behind the snowbanks, the parking lot was deserted, but he parked at the curb, beneath a faded pink neon sign that spelled out the name of the restaurant.

"Kon iki?" Paulette murmured, reading the sign aloud.

Jonathan hunched over the wheel so that he could see the sign through the windshield. "It's supposed to be Tiki."

She peered at the sign again and recognized her mistake. "Of course," she said. "The *T*'s burned out." She studied Jonathan curiously as he opened her door. "Where did you hear about this place?"

"One of my clients asked me to check it out."

"As a tax write-off?"

Jonathan grinned. "Would you rather go somewhere else?"

She leaped out of the car before he'd finished speaking. "No, this'll be an adventure."

The exterior of Kon-Tiki looked like a Wisconsin farmhouse, circa 1930. The interior was a Midwestern version of a grass shack.

A lush jungle of greenery swamped the reception area. The walls were bamboo-paneled, and woven straw mats carpeted the floor. The hostess was slim and soft-spoken, with exotic dark eyes and jeweled combs tucked into her hair. They barely had time to remove their coats before she bade them "Aloha," and showed them to a table beside a small fountain.

"Not much of a crowd," said Jonathan, surveying the room. Only three other tables were occupied.

"No, sir, not tonight. But the service is superb."

The hostess took their drink orders and hurried toward the bar before he could ask about the quality of the food, but another young woman, who might have been the hostess's twin, took her place.

"My name's Mei Ling, and I'll be your waitress," she said. She recited the menu and by the time she finished describing the lychee duck, the hostess had returned with their drinks.

There was nothing extraordinary about Jonathan's gin and tonic, but Paulette had ordered one of the house specials, and it was spectacular. Served in a ceramic pineapple mug, it was garnished with three kinds of fruit, a sprig of artificial orchids and a miniature parasol.

"It's almost as flamboyant as you are," said Jonathan.

Paulette laughed. "Now I know why they call it a Carmen Miranda. I'm not sure whether to drink it or wear it on my head."

Jonathan cocked an eyebrow at her. "Are you sure you shouldn't use it for perfume?"

"That's an interesting notion. I'll take it under advisement."

He grinned as a new idea occurred to him. "Actually, I think you should be wearing a lei and a sarong."

"Do you really?"

"To be honest, no."

She smiled and patted his hand. "That's okay, Jack. Some of my best friends are conventional."

"I'm sure they are. Otherwise they might upstage you."

Her smile froze. She jerked her hand away as if she had touched a live coal, and Jonathan could have kicked himself.

Why hadn't he kept his opinion to himself? He'd meant to charm Paulette, not offend her. "Look, I'm sorry—" he began.

"No, Jack, I'm the one who should apologize."

"What for? I have no business criticizing you."

"Granted, but in this case I asked for it. I was being smug and superior—" She lapsed into silence and squared her shoulders. "The truth is, there's something about you that makes me feel defensive. You're so organized—*together*—controlled—"

"You make me sound boring."

"I don't mean to. Really I don't. I admire your efficiency. I mean, look at you! Even your clothes are coordinated."

Jonathan leaned back in his chair. "I'm afraid you lost me. What do clothes have to do with being organized?"

"They're a symbol, don't you see?" Her expression intent, Paulette reached across the table and flapped the ends of his necktie under his nose. "From what I've seen of you, you're appropriately dressed whatever the occasion. Your clothes are well thought-out and beautifully cared for, but I'll bet you don't waste time worrying about what you're going to wear. Your wardrobe is planned. It's orderly. And so is the rest of your life."

Jonathan studied her speculatively, wondering if she was putting him on. "Don't you think you're oversimplifying?"

"Not me," she answered. "I'm good at complicating matters, not simplifying them. For some reason, things never turn out the way I plan."

"Seems to me that's not an unmixed blessing, Paulette. If you could predict what's going to happen tomorrow—or next week, or next month—would you want to?"

"No, but there are times when it'd be nice to know what's going to happen in the next five minutes."

"That's easy," he said. "Five minutes from now you'll be finishing your drink and telling me about yourself."

At his coaxing, Paulette separated the drinking straw from the fruit salad in her mug and took an obliging sip.

"How is it?" he asked.

"Not bad."

"*What* is it?"

She took another sip. "Rum and pineapple, I think. Also coconut." She took a third sip. "It's kind of like a piña colada, only more potent." After a fourth sip, she declared, "I have this overwhelming urge to play the marimba."

"Have some more," said Jonathan. "It'll pass."

He was too busy trying to charm Paulette to notice that she had diverted the conversation. They were eating their salads before he repeated his suggestion that she tell him about herself.

She paused in the act of buttering a roll. "What would you like to know?"

He wanted to know if she only dated jocks and married men, but he couldn't ask about her love life without some sort of buildup. Brief as their acquaintance was, he believed he had Paulette pegged. Everything indicated she was a thrill-seeker in search of the ultimate emotional high. She was brighter than he'd thought—or at least more clever—but chances were she had a short attention span and about as much depth as sheet ice in July.

Which meant he'd get further if he showed a little finesse. He needed to dazzle her with his footwork, stay one step ahead of her—

"How much do you weigh?"

He blurted out the question, hoping to catch her off balance. For a moment he thought he'd succeeded. Paulette lost her grip on the butter knife and it clattered onto her plate.

"What is this, Jack? Some kind of test?"

"It's just a game my brother and I used to play. We called it 'Truth or Consequences.'"

"What are the consequences if I don't tell the truth?"

"I'm not sure, because I never risked lying. My brother had me convinced my nose would grow if I did. But if you're sensitive about your weight, you don't have to answer."

Paulette lowered her eyelids with a coquettish flutter of lashes. "Should I be sensitive about it?"

With an invitation like that, Jonathan could not resist looking her over, and while his gaze traced the enticing lines from her neck to her shoulders, then to the sweet roundness of her bosom, she stole the cherry tomato from his salad.

"The last time I stepped on the scales I weighed a hundred and five." She smiled guiltily and touched the tip of her nose. "Well, maybe a hundred eight, but not an ounce more."

Content that she had won round one, she popped the tomato into her mouth and wiped her hands on her napkin.

"Now, Jack, I hope you'll agree that turnabout's fair play."

"Absolutely," he said. "Take your best shot."

For perhaps half a minute Paulette was silent. From the ghost of a smile that played about her lips, he decided she was savoring her triumph. But he was willing to concede this minor skirmish as long as he won the war.

"Managing other people's investments must be fairly lucrative." She ventured this remark casually, as if it were only of passing interest. Then came the zinger. "How much do you earn a year?"

"More than a locksmith but less than my clients," he shot back. "How about you?"

"Enough to keep you in popcorn. Do you like your work?"

"If I didn't, I'd get into something else. As a general rule, I try not to do things I don't enjoy."

"Bravo, Jack! That's something we have in common."

"Then I take it you like being the Shorewood registrar."

"*Assistant* registrar," Paulette qualified. "And yes, I like my work. I meet interesting people, it's fun working with the students, and since I'm not the department chairman, I don't have to contend with the hassles of establishing policy and administering it."

"But wouldn't you like the recognition?"

"Not if I have to pay for it with headaches."

Gotcha! thought Jonathan. He drank the last of his gin and tonic, confident that he had found the weak spot in her facade. "You know, Paulette, that sounds suspiciously like sour grapes to me."

"Well, it's not." She flushed a vivid pink. Warning lights danced in her eyes. "This may surprise you, Jack, but I'm good at what I do—"

"Naturally you are. If you weren't, you wouldn't enjoy it."

"Right on. And I've had my share of opportunities for advancement. Just last fall, for instance, I was offered the registrar's job at a college in Milwaukee. It would've meant more money, more prestige—"

"And you turned it down. May I ask why?"

Paulette shrugged and snitched the last forkful of lettuce from his plate. "I guess I'm just not hungry for power."

"I see," said Jonathan. But he wasn't buying Paulette's excuse. She had claimed she wasn't hungry for dinner either, yet she had polished off her salad and most of his as well.

Mei Ling arrived at their table with a tray of steaming serving dishes, and they called a time out while she filled Jonathan's plate with mahimahi and succulent slices of barbecued pork and a vegetable dish with an unpronounceable name made with snow peas, water chestnuts, celery and mushrooms, topped with slivered almonds.

"Looks delicious," Paulette observed.

"Tastes it, too," said Jonathan. "Are you sure you wouldn't like to order something?"

"No, thanks. I couldn't eat another bite." But after a few minutes of watching him enjoy the meal, she changed her mind. "Maybe I'll have a wonton or two. And a little of the fried rice."

"You should try the pea pods."

"You talked me into it."

Would that she were always so easily swayed, Jonathan thought. Aloud, he said, "It's a good thing Mei Ling left an extra plate."

Paulette nodded, watching eagerly as he spooned vegetables onto her plate. "By the way," she said, "that's four questions you owe me."

"It's only three, but who's counting?"

"Not me," said Paulette. "With all this lovely food and the Carmen Miranda, I'm feeling much too mellow to keep score."

This was it, Jonathan realized. The perfect opening. The moment he had been waiting for.

"Tell me, Paulette, how do you feel about marriage?"

"Marriage?" She repeated the word as if it were alien to her. "Well, everybody's doing it, aren't they? And they have been ever since Noah, so I guess it can't be all bad."

Paulette paused for a bite of wonton. Her face was pensive as she continued. "Going through life two by two seems to be the natural order of things. Swans and geese do it. Lions do it. Even Santa's reindeer do it. Rudolph's an exception, of course, but he's not part of the original cast. He's the latecomer, the nonconformist, the comic relief. He's out of step with the others, and to the extent that he breaks stride, he reaffirms their traditions. . . ."

Jonathan had expected a straightforward answer to a personal question, not a philosophical discourse on pair-bonding. He listened with growing confusion, and at the first opportunity, he interrupted.

"Excuse me, I guess I didn't make myself clear. What I mean is, would you yourself like to get married?"

Paulette stared at him, wide-eyed with disbelief. "Jack, I don't know what to say, except that I'm touched. Really I am...."

Jonathan broke out in a sweat. His life flashed before his eyes. *Good Lord, this couldn't be happening! She couldn't think he had proposed!*

"You're very sweet, and you've done me a great honor, but I—"

"Don't, Paulette. You've said enough. You needn't explain."

"But I don't want to hurt your feelings—"

"You won't. Believe me, you won't."

"Well, as long as you understand. The truth is, we hardly know each other—"

He pressed his forefinger to her lips. "Please, Paulette. Not another word."

Her eyes shied away from his. "I need to powder my nose," she mumbled, groping for her purse.

She bolted for the ladies' room, leaving Jonathan slumped over the table, shaken by his narrow escape.

He had come close to proposing once before, to his college sweetheart, Jocelyn. He'd even bought the ring. But at the last minute, he'd decided marriage would have to wait until he had established his business. While he was making a name for himself, Jocelyn was making it with his brother, and by the time he'd had sufficient income to support a wife, Jocelyn and Larry were engaged.

When he'd heard about their engagement, he'd felt like a reject, and he was dismayed to realize he felt the same way now, even though he knew marriage was out of the question.

Paulette and he were wrong for each other. They were fire and ice, impulse and reason, mismatched in every respect.

But life with her would never be dull. She made him laugh, and she was delightfully unpredictable; the most exciting woman he'd met in ages. He envied the man she would marry.

Jonathan thought of her knowing green eyes, her husky laugh. He imagined the taste of her lips, the feel of her skin, the silken texture of coppery hair fanned across her pillow, and a surge of desire rose in him; a need so compelling that he had to admit, after a few hours in Paulette's company, the fine line between a slip of the tongue and a Freudian slip was beginning to blur.

Chapter Five

"What am I going to do, Annie? I've made such a mess of things."

"Take a deep breath, Paulette. Try to calm down."

"Calm down!" Paulette's hand tightened around the receiver of the pay phone. "How can I calm down when I've made an idiot of myself? I've never been so embarrassed in my life."

The mirrored walls of the powder room reflected her distress, and she averted her gaze, shutting out the image of the frantic, red-faced fool she had become. She wished she could disappear, that the ground would open up and swallow her. She wished she had never been born.

"It's going to be all right, Paulette. Honestly. I know things seem pretty grim just now, but someday you'll look back at this and laugh."

"I don't care about someday. All I care about is tonight. How could I have been so stupid?"

"Don't be so hard on yourself. You made a mistake, that's all."

"You're wrong, Annie. If you cross the street against the light and a Mack truck runs over you, that's a mistake. When you're having dinner with a man who's a virtual stranger and he asks a polite question about marriage and you leap to the conclusion that he's proposed, that's a *disaster*!"

Tears stung Paulette's eyes. She choked back a sob. "Oh, God! If you'd seen Jack's face. He was horrified when it dawned on him that I'd misinterpreted things. And then at the end, he looked as if I'd granted him a stay of execution."

"At least you said no."

"But it was so humiliating." She turned away from the mirrors, resting her forehead against the cool metallic casing on the telephone. "P-please, Annie. I'm begging you. Won't you come get me?"

"You mean you're not at your apartment?"

"No, I'm phoning from the restaurant, and I don't have any money. I must've left my billfold at home. I had to borrow a quarter from Mei Ling to call you."

"Who's Mei Ling?"

"Our waitress."

"Well, where's Jack?"

"Still at the table, I guess. But there's no way I can face him again."

"I'm afraid you'll have to, Paulette. You live in the same building. You can't avoid him forever."

"Yes, I can. I'll move out of the studio. I'll leave town—"

"Listen, sweetie, I realize you're terribly upset, but before you rush off the deep end, why not put this in perspective."

"P-perspective?"

"That's right. For example, have you given any consideration to Jack's point of view?"

"Dammit, Annie, that's *all* I can think of. I wish to God I could forget Jonathan Day and his pompous point of view."

"Of course you do, dear. That's only natural. But has it occurred to you that he might think you only pretended to misunderstand him?"

"Wait a minute. What are you saying?"

"Just that, as far as he knows, everything you did, everything you said might have been carefully orchestrated."

"That's ridiculous. Why would I pull such a stunt?"

"You tell me, Paulette. Why'd you pull similar stunts in the past?"

There was an eloquent silence. Paulette's spirits rose. "I might have been teasing," she said. "It could've been a practical joke."

"Exactly," said Anne. "Or you might've pretended to misunderstand him for its shock value."

"So you think I should brazen it out?"

"I think you should be yourself."

"Same difference." Paulette took a deep breath and ran her fingers through her hair. "I suppose I'd better get back to the table before Jack gets suspicious."

"I'd say that's a good plan," Anne replied. "And chin up, Paulette. If all else fails, think of those old Doris Day movies you're always watching and remember: Nothing devastating will happen as long as you keep both feet on the floor."

AN AGITATED PAULETTE had gone to the ladies' room; a subdued Paulette returned. Neither she nor Jonathan said much until they were preparing to leave the restaurant, and then she asked him to add an extra quarter to Mei Ling's tip.

"I borrowed twenty-five cents for a phone call," Paulette explained. She didn't volunteer whom the call was to, and Jonathan didn't ask.

They were in the car, speeding along University Avenue, before she spoke again.

"What will you tell your client about Kon-Tiki?"

"I'll tell him it has great food, excellent service, plenty of atmosphere and a lousy location."

"Then you'll recommend against the investment."

Jonathan shook his head. "It's not that cut-and-dried, Paulette. The state highway department has plans to widen the beltline, so it figures, if the legislature votes to fund the expansion, and if the project is constructed along the proposed blue line, a few years from now Kon-Tiki could be situated on a major interchange."

"Those are some big ifs."

"It's a gamble, all right, but the odds are considerably better than the chances of filling an inside straight, and at the price the owner's asking, the property could pay handsome dividends. It could be a very sweet deal. I'll have to give it some thought."

Paulette studied Jonathan's face by the lights of the oncoming traffic. "You love it, don't you? The wheeling and dealing. You like it even more because it involves an element of risk."

"It's a calculated risk, but yes, since you mention it, I've always welcomed a challenge." A squeal of brakes punctuated this comment. The sports car fishtailed to a stop at a red light, and Jonathan slanted a grin her way. "You know, Paulette, earlier this evening I was thinking that you're a thrill-seeker. I guess maybe I'm one too, at least as far as investments are concerned."

"There's no comparison, Jack. You're much more of a daredevil than I am. I might bend the rules of decorum here and there, but I abide by the laws of nature. I'd certainly never dream of trying to break the land-speed barrier."

Jonathan took the hint. He stayed within the speed limit the rest of the way home.

When they arrived at the apartment building, he invited her in for coffee.

"I thought you had work to do," she said.

"It'll keep."

Faced with such enthusiasm, how could she say no?

She stood in the entryway while he took her coat and hung it in the guest closet, and then, with a gentle push at the small of her back, he guided her toward the living room.

"Make yourself at home," he said. "I'll only be a minute."

While he started the coffee, she sat on the sofa, thinking of all the reasons she shouldn't be there. Although it was only nine-thirty, she'd hardly closed her eyes the night before, and she was sleepy. She'd had a full day, and since she had postponed several of her own chores to shop for Jonathan's Christmas tree, tomorrow promised to be even more hectic.

She had last-minute presents to buy, gift wrapping to finish, cookies to bake for the senior citizens' center. And then she had to deliver her gifts and do some grocery shopping. She also had to stop at a hardware store and buy some cookware. But first she had better pick up a rental car, because she couldn't manage all those errands if she relied on the Metro buses.

The frosting on the cake was that she had told Jonathan she would decorate the spruce, but at least she'd had the foresight to take the next couple of days off.

With the holiday weekend coming up, that gave her five days to tie up the loose ends in her life.

She yawned and lounged back against the upholstery. The length of the sofa beckoned her; the cushions invited her to lie down and close her eyes, just for a few seconds. Even the aroma of coffee that wafted from the kitchen didn't dispel her weariness.

I should have gone straight upstairs, she thought. *Straight to bed.* And she resolved that, for the sake of being neighborly, she would have one cup of coffee. After that, she would bid Jonathan good-night.

But once the coffee was brewed and Jonathan brought it into the living room, she forgot how drowsy she was. He asked if she used sugar or cream, and she said, "No, I take it black."

"That's something else we have in common," he said, and there was an undercurrent of tension in his reply that made her wonder if he had something more than a friendly cup of coffee on his mind. But her suspicions were fleeting, lulled by his smile.

"So tell me," she said, "how long have you had this delusion that you're Mario Andretti?"

Jonathan's grin broadened. He sat beside her on the couch, and they started exchanging information, searching for points where their backgrounds converged, and by the time her coffee cup was empty, Paulette had forgotten her intention to say good-night.

He told her he was a fifth-generation Westerner, and that his great-great-grandparents had been pioneer settlers in the Pacific Northwest. He said, "I was born in the same house, in the same bed where my grandfather was born."

"What happened to your father?" she asked.

"He was born in the hospital. Grandma had to have a cesarean delivery."

"Are your grandparents still living?"

"They are, and they're still in Seattle, along with the rest of the clan. I'm considered a maverick because I pulled up stakes and moved to Wisconsin."

"Why did you?"

"Partly for location. My work requires a certain amount of mobility, and it's easy to get to either the East coast or the West from Madison."

"And the other part?"

"Well, with a couple dozen relatives waiting to prop me up if my business slumped, I began to feel smothered. I guess I needed to prove I could make it on my own."

"You must be the youngest," said Paulette.

"Of my generation," Jonathan answered. "Since I left home Laurence and his wife have had a baby boy, and there are also some younger cousins who have come of age."

"Is Laurence the brother who conned you into believing *Pinocchio* was a true story?"

"He is. He's also my only brother." Jonathan refilled her cup and returned the carafe to its trivet. "How about you, Paulette? Are you from a large family?"

"Nope. No grandparents, no great-grandparents, no aunts or uncles or cousins. Just my dad and mother, my sister Nicole and me. And we moved five times before I started kindergarten. The condo was the first place I lived long enough to see the trees grow."

"Is your father in the military or something?"

"Or something," she said. "He's a minister."

"You mean he's a diplomat, like with morning coats and garden parties and the foreign service?"

"No, I mean he's an Episcopal priest, like with vestments and potluck suppers and morning and evening services."

Jonathan looked at her as if the tip of her nose had sprouted an extra inch. "You're putting me on."

"Not about this," she replied dryly. "Till I was four I thought all the kids at Sunday school were my brothers and sisters because they called my daddy Father. And incidentally, for a long time I was considered the black sheep because I spent a year between high school and college hitchhiking cross-country."

"Are you still the black sheep?"

"Of course. I have a reputation to maintain. My parents might not recognize me if I reformed."

"But they must've been worried sick by your hitchhiking."

"That was the general idea," said Paulette. "Not that I admitted it at the time."

"I'm surprised you hadn't had enough traveling."

He was still staring at her nose. Or was it her mouth he found so fascinating?

"Well, you see," she replied, "we moved practically every year, but most of the moves were from one part of Minneapolis to another. They weren't connected to my father's ministry."

"What were they connected to?"

"My mother's quest for the ideal house."

Jonathan frowned, but he didn't look away from her mouth, and she began to feel self-conscious. When she moistened her lips, he mimicked the movement. She tore her gaze away from his, but her treacherous memory would not let her forget that erotic sweep of his tongue.

"Didn't your dad's congregation provide a house as part of his salary?"

Jonathan's voice had dropped an octave. It was as if he were communicating on two levels; one vocal and platonic, the other silent and provocative.

She leaned forward and set her cup on the coffee table, hoping to keep her distance from him, but he took advantage of her pretext by occupying the space behind her, filling it with his arm, his shoulder, half of his chest. She felt the cushions give beneath his weight and realized if she sat back now, she would be in his embrace, and heaven knew where that might lead.

"They did provide a house," she replied, "but it was huge and drafty, impossible to heat in the winter and ugly as sin. After a few months of trying to make it livable, my mother talked the vestry into selling the place and letting her use the proceeds to buy a new rectory. Only the property didn't sell for much, which meant the new rectory was not a big improvement. But she painted and papered and fixed the roof and refinished the woodwork, and a year later the church sold that house at a profit, so we moved into another white elephant, in a slightly better neighborhood, and the painting and papering started all over again."

"She showed them the value of gentrification," said Jonathan.

"I wouldn't have put it in quite those terms, but yes, I guess that's what she did."

"When did the vestry realize it had a money-making proposition on its hands?"

"Not right away. The church was in a fringe area. Most of the parishioners were retirement age, and the younger families tended to be transient. As they became more affluent, they moved to the suburbs and took their tithes with them, which left Dad's parish on a shaky foundation financially. Before my mother came into their lives, they'd been subsidized by the diocese for so long, it took them a while to recognize they were out of the red."

"They should've put her on salary."

"They tried to, but she turned them down. She said it was a labor of love—her contribution to her husband's ministry."

"Interesting," Jonathan murmured.

And a lot to live up to, thought Paulette.

"What did they do when she found her ideal house?"

"Nothing. She's still looking."

Paulette sounded so disgruntled that Jonathan chuckled. She felt the laughter rumble up from his chest and realized how close he was, but when she tried to inch forward, his arm fastened about her waist.

"Relax," he whispered. "I won't bite. Not unless you want me to, and not where it would show."

It hadn't occurred to her that Jonathan would take such liberties. It hadn't occurred to her that she would *want* him to. But now that he had brought up the subject— She dug her heels into the carpet and tried to ease away again, but his hand spanned her midriff. With her slightest movement forward, his thumb made an electrifying groove just beneath her breast, and the sensational possibilities this brought to mind convinced her that escape was more dangerous than staying put.

She sat motionless, but not unresponsive, deceived by Jonathan's proper exterior and by her own false assumptions, seduced by the way he was nuzzling her ear and by the exquisite glide of his hand along her inner arm.

He followed her arm to her shoulder, her shoulder to her spine, and her spine to the nape of her neck. He brushed the backs of his fingers against her cheek as if he were testing the softness of her skin, and she realized Doris Day was wrong. A man like Jack could do devastating things to a woman, even if she did keep both feet on the floor.

Why fight it? A delicious lassitude possessed her; she hadn't the strength to resist.

He felt the tension leave her body, felt her go slack and pliant, and drew her into his arms. She turned to him, lifting her mouth for his kiss. In her eagerness, she barked her shin on the coffee table. She gasped with pain, and from the corner of her eye saw the carafe of coffee slide off the trivet onto the edge of the table. It teetered there for a moment, as if it might defy gravity, but before she could call out a warning, the carafe sailed off the table, spilling its contents over Jonathan's foot.

He howled with pain. In less than an instant he had peeled off his shoe and sock and was hobbling toward the bathroom, trailing curses behind him. When Paulette caught up with him, he was standing in the tub, running cold water over his foot and ankle.

"Are you all right?"

He snarled something about "damfool questions." She took it to mean he had things under control and loitered in the doorway until concern overcame trepidation.

"Can I get you anything?"

He muttered something about "ditsy redheads." She took it as an invitation and sat on the rim of the tub, contemplating his foot, waiting until the skin had gone from lobster-red to a cooler, less ominous pink.

"It looks much better already, don't you think?"

He glared morosely at his foot and mumbled something about "brain-dead jocks." She took this to mean he would rather be left alone.

"Well," she said uneasily, wondering if she should offer to sponge the coffee stains out of the carpet, "I guess I should be leaving."

Jonathan didn't protest. She wanted to remind him that this accident was not entirely her fault. She wanted to say she was sorry. She wanted to tell him if he had to blame someone, he should blame himself. But it seemed safer not to say anything until she had reached the hall.

She turned for one more look at him, and had to force back a bubble of laughter. Now that the emergency was over, she was struck by how comical he looked, balancing storklike in the tub, one shoe off and one shoe on, still wearing his banker's-gray trousers and sport jacket, his dress shirt and tie.

She cleared her throat to get his attention, and when his scrutiny shifted from his foot to her, she inquired, "Are you by any chance related to Doris Day?"

"She changed her name," he answered with quiet dignity. "Originally, I believe it was von Kappelhoff. Why do you ask?"

"No reason." She gave him a tentative smile and took a backward step, away from the door.

"Not so fast, Paulette." He hopped out of the tub and limped toward her. "Will I see you tomorrow?"

"That depends. Will you behave yourself?"

"Will you?"

She smiled again, less tentatively. "Que sarà, sarà."

Chapter Six

The first of the poinsettias arrived the next morning, just as Paulette was leaving to pick up her rental car. Two more were delivered early that afternoon, while she was up to her elbows in cookie dough, and by six that evening she had received three more poinsettias, an azalea and a cyclamen.

At seven o'clock, her errands completed, she knocked at Jonathan's door.

"Paulette-the-tree-trimmer reporting for duty." She gave him a jaunty salute, and he grinned as he ushered her inside.

"Have you eaten?"

She told him she had, glancing around the living room. Jonathan's mail—mostly Christmas cards from the look of the envelopes—littered one end of the coffee table. An open pizza carton filled the other.

"If I'm interrupting your supper I can come back later," she said.

"No, this is fine. I'm on my last slice."

She watched surreptitiously as he returned to his chair and was relieved that she detected no hesitation in his stride. The plush gray carpeting was spotless, too. Apparently last night's mishap with the coffee pot had left no residue, except that tonight he was drinking milk.

"If you're sure you don't mind," she said, "I would like to get started stringing the lights."

"My spruce is your spruce," Jonathan replied with a magnanimous sweep of his hand. "I left all the stuff by the tree."

She sorted through the shopping bags while he finished his pizza, and by the time he carried the empty carton to the kitchen, she had unraveled the wiring on the minilights and was preparing to arrange them on the tree.

"Hold on a sec," said Jonathan. "There's been a slight change of plan." He made a detour past the coat closet and pulled a florist's box from the shelf.

"What's this?" she inquired as he offered her the box.

"I picked up some doves for the top. Let me put them on, then we can rig the lights around them."

He dragged a step stool out of the pantry and positioned it near the spruce, and one by one, she handed him the feathery white doves, kibitzing while he fastened them to the topmost branches.

"Now, Paulette, if you'll plug in the lights, we'll see what we have."

She did as Jonathan directed, then stepped back and applauded the halo effect of lights shimmering through the wings.

"They're lovely, Jack. Really lovely. But what made you think of doves? Are they one of your traditions?"

"No. My family uses a star at the top."

"A symbol of high expectations," she murmured.

"Could be. And I'll bet your folks use an angel."

"What else?"

Jonathan laughed. "You realize this means we're the offspring of overachievers."

Paulette nodded. "I prefer the doves."

"So do I."

Their gazes met and melded, and for the moment it seemed their feelings had found the harmony signified by the doves. Then Jonathan climbed off the stool so that he could distribute the lights on the lower branches, and after handing him the next string, Paulette began removing the candy canes from their packaging.

In the thirty minutes since her arrival, Jonathan hadn't mentioned work. She marveled at his newly cooperative attitude, but decided not to question him about it. After all, why rock the boat?

They shared a companionable silence until he asked how she had spent her day. She told him about the shopping and baking, and the Ford Escort she had rented.

"I saw the car in the driveway," Jonathan said. "How do you like it?"

Paulette shrugged. The Escort got her where she wanted to go more quickly and with much more convenience than the bus. Anything else was a matter of indifference to her. She had to return it by noon tomorrow in any case, but the process of renting the Escort had sparked another idea.

"I also stopped at Colortyme and rented some furniture for the studio," she said. "You know—a daybed, a chest of drawers, a dinette set, that sort of thing. They'll be delivered next Tuesday. And while I was at it, I bought a couple of floor lamps, and the pièce de résistance, a TV set."

"You seem more excited about the television than you are about the car."

"What if I am? A car's just transportation, but a TV is—well, it's entertainment."

Jonathan shot her an inquiring glance. "I might've known you'd put a premium on pleasure."

Paulette opened her mouth to defend herself, then spotted the telltale quirk of his lips and made a face at him instead.

"To each his own," she replied airily. "You get your kicks from offtrack racing, I get mine from watching old movies."

"What, no *Dynasty*? No *Wheel of Fortune*?"

"Sometimes. But given the choice, I prefer Joan Crawford to Joan Collins."

"Why? What's the big attraction of the golden oldies?"

"I'm not sure. Maybe it's simply the difference between theatrical movies and the shows they make for TV, or maybe it's sheer escapism, but I think the old-time stars have more grit, more glitz, more glamour. The characters they played were larger than life—"

"They were heroic, all right," Jonathan allowed.

"Yes, they were. And at the same time they seemed more *real*. This afternoon, for instance, I caught the end of *Miracle on 34th Street*—"

"I'm surprised you haven't seen it before."

"I have, Jack. Every Christmas for as long as I can remember. And every time I see it, it brings back memories of Christmases past."

"What kind of memories?"

"All kinds. Happy ones. Sad ones. Today it made me recall how wonderful it was to believe in Santa Claus and the Easter Bunny and the tooth fairy—all those childish fantasies. But I also recalled how awful it was to lose faith."

"That's life, Paulette. It's part of the price a person pays for growing up."

"I realize that, but still, it's sad. If you think about it, it's like the first loss of innocence."

Jonathan untangled the last string of lights and wove it through the spruce boughs to the far side of the tree. "When did you stop believing?" he asked.

"I suppose it was the year I thought my mother and father were giving me a Chatty Cathy doll."

"What do you mean, you thought they were giving you the doll?"

"Just that." Paulette draped several strands of red velvet ribbon about her neck, climbed onto the step stool and tied a big, floppy bow on one of the branches. Her expression was wistful as she said, "You probably don't remember Chatty Cathy."

"Just the name," said Jonathan. "I wasn't into dolls."

"Well, take it from me, she was adorable. She had a brown ponytail and eyes that opened and shut and a darling dress with puffy sleeves and a full skirt, but best of all, she could talk!"

Jonathan smiled. "I assumed as much from her name. What did she say?"

"Things like 'Would you like to play with me? Would you like to be my friend?'" Paulette sighed. "I'm telling you, Jack, I'd never wanted anything as much as I wanted Chatty Cathy. I wrote a letter to Santa and taped her picture from the Sears catalog above my bed and yearned over her in store windows and prayed for her every night."

"How old were you?"

"Seven. And for two whole months I was a model child. I behaved so well, my parents thought I must be coming down with something. Then one day I came upon my mother's cache of presents, and I couldn't resist peeking. I had to know if I was getting Chatty Cathy."

"But the doll wasn't there?"

"She was there," Paulette declared flatly, "and I was overjoyed. I could hardly contain myself. I don't think I slept a wink that Christmas Eve. But then, on Christmas morning I found out my parents had given the doll to one of the little girls in my Sunday School class."

"Why'd they do that? Were they always so generous with their parishioners?"

"No, not always. They couldn't afford to be. But her father was out of work, and I suppose Chatty Cathy was all the Christmas she had."

"You poor kid. You must've been heartbroken."

"I don't know about heartbroken, but I was royally peeved, and I made no effort to hide my resentment, even though my mother did her darnedest to console me. I remember her talking about the true meaning of Christmas, telling me, 'It's more blessed to give than receive.'"

"Not much comfort for a seven-year-old."

"You can say that again. But I got even. Mother and Dad gave me a chemistry set that year, and the first thing I mixed was ammonium sulfate. The rectory smelled like rotten eggs for a week."

Jonathan grinned, not so much from amusement at Paulette's revenge, but because he could picture her at seven, dressed in Mary Janes and a ruffled pinafore, with freckles on her nose and scabs on her knees, an angelic gap-toothed smile and an imp of mischief in her eyes.

"I can identify with that," he said. "The major disappointment of my childhood was that I always wanted a dog."

"And you never got one?"

"Nope. My mom's allergic to them. But I guess my most memorable Christmas was the year I got a toboggan."

"Oh? Why's that?"

"Because the first time I took it out I tangled with a fence post and broke my arm."

Jonathan hooked the last light in place and circled the tree, surveying his handiwork, moving an occasional bulb a few millimeters up or down to the right or to the left, until they were precisely balanced. When he was satisfied with the symmetry of the lights, he picked up one of the ribbons and tied it on the tree, but unlike Paulette's uninhibited loops and long, flowing streamers, his arrangement was stiff and spiky, as if he were knotting a bow tie.

Paulette sank her teeth into her upper lip, telling herself she would not object, until he tied on another ribbon. Then she decided that was two too many.

"Why don't you do the snowflakes, Jack? Let me take care of the ribbons."

"Fine by me." He sat on his haunches and foraged through the decorations in the shopping bag, but he bypassed the crocheted snowflakes when he discovered a packet of hunting horns. "Oh, wow! I'd rather do these."

His eyes were alight with eagerness as he tore off the molded plastic wrapper and removed one of the horns. He held the mouthpiece to his lips and blew an experimental puff of air through it, and it gave off a high-pitched toot.

"How about that? It actually works!"

He blew through the mouthpiece again, forcefully, repetitiously, two longs and a short, and Paulette recognized the tune he was playing: "Jingle Bells."

Smiling, she said, "Okay, Jonny-one-note. You do the horns."

He gave her a sheepish grin and peeled off the rest of the plastic wrap. "Listen, Paulette, I've got an idea. We're about through here and it's barely nine o'clock—"

"Shank of the evening," she said.

"Right. So why don't we go tobogganing?"

His suggestion caught her unprepared. The bow she was working on came out lopsided, but in the seconds it took her to retie the ribbon, she recovered.

"You know, Jack, sometimes you amaze me."

His grin wavered. "The feeling's mutual, but does that mean you'd rather not go?"

"No, just the opposite. I'd love to go tobogganing with you—on one condition."

"Name it."

"We take my car."

"It's a deal," said Jonathan, springing to his feet. "I'll leave the driving to you, Paulette, as long as I get to be captain of the toboggan."

She agreed, of course. There was no reason not to. She hadn't done a lot of sledding, but she knew very well that to all intents and purposes a toboggan steered itself. A passenger might be required to make minor corrections by banking a hand off the snow, but the terrain and the condition of the hillside took care of the rest. There was no need for a captain.

A few minutes later Paulette returned to the studio and got into jeans, leg warmers and moon boots without stopping to consider whether she should dress for warmth or fashion. The fire had eliminated that concern.

She was putting on an oversize sweater patterned in an artist's palette of lilac, violet and periwinkle blue before it occurred to her that she was finally going to see Jonathan in something other than gray pinstripes. But when they rendezvoused downstairs, she found that though he had changed his stripes, his hiking boots, ski bib, pullover and waist-length jacket were a conservative gunmetal gray. Just two things kept him from blending into the shadows: a pair of aviator glasses, and the fringed, ivory silk scarf he had wound about his neck.

"As I live and breathe, it's the Red Baron in the flesh!"

Jonathan seemed pleased by the comparison. "Flattery will get you everywhere, Paulette."

"It's not flattery," she said, and she meant it. He looked dashing, daring, and more dangerous than the Red Baron. While they were loading the toboggan onto the roof of the Escort, she told herself that seeing this facet of his personality was worth the wait.

They went to a park on the far west side of town, where the hills were lofty and the floodlights burned all night.

"It's a great evening to be outdoors," Jonathan remarked as they pulled into the parking area.

Paulette thought he was right. The temperature was in the twenties, the sky was starry and crisp, and the pristine white slopes that formed half of a natural amphitheater were dotted with sledders and skiers and children on snow saucers, in a scene reminiscent of Currier and Ives.

A hockey game was in progress on one of the skating rinks. They stopped to watch the rough-and-tumble play for a few minutes, until one of the teams scored. Jonathan adjusted his glasses, and Paulette put on her earmuffs and mittens before they moved on, towing the wooden toboggan between them.

From the bottom the sledding hill didn't seem particularly steep, but halfway to the top a pair of teenagers whizzed by at a breathtaking speed, and Paulette realized the incline was more precipitous than she'd thought.

The view from the summit was intimidating.

In the safety of the parking lot she had estimated the distance to the crest as several hundred yards; while they waited their turn to take off, she doubled her estimate. They had climbed so high, the hockey players looked the size of munchkins. What was more, while the snow on the ski trails was powdery and groomed, the sledding hill was a giant's washboard of bumps and jumps and glacial whoop-de-dos.

The boy ahead of them in line, a snub-nosed ten-year-old with hair like shredded wheat, struck up a conversation with Jonathan.

"Mister," he said, "that's one gnarly toboggan."

"I'll bet it's not as fast as your snow tube," Jonathan replied.

They debated the merits of various types of sleds until the slope below them was clear, and then the boy tossed his inner tube down and did a belly flop across it.

"Geronimo!" he hollered, and plummeted toward the parking lot like a rocket gone out of control.

Paulette had a mild phobia for heights, so this performance was enough to make the color drain from her face, but Jonathan gave her no time for second thoughts. He had dragged the toboggan to the brow of the ridge, and as soon as the run was clear he signaled her to get aboard.

She hesitated, and he smiled. "You're not going to chicken out on me, are you?"

She answered with a shake of her head, and took her place at the front of the toboggan, clinging for dear life to the ropes at either side. Jonathan bent over her from behind and reached around her waist for secure handholds on the ropes. She closed her eyes as he gave the toboggan a practice shove or two. His breath stirred the hair at the crown of her head as he said, "Little kids take this hill all the time, Paulette, so don't worry about a thing. We'll go easy on the first run."

He took a few running steps. She felt his biceps flex, felt the power in his forearms as he gave a final shove. With the same lithe motion, he swung onto the toboggan, and then they were coasting, gaining momentum, hurtling downhill in a blistering rush. Her heart catapulted into her throat and there was a strange hollow feeling where her stomach should have been; it was exhilarating and scary and *fun*.

"Lean right," Jonathan prompted. "Hang on!"

She followed his lead as if they were dancing, gauging her movements from his. The toboggan swerved, and she gripped the rope so fiercely, her fingers went numb. She tried to open her eyes, but after a blurry glimpse of snowdrifts and sky, she closed them tight again.

At the bottom of the grade the toboggan shot off the edge of a snowbank and went flying through the air in an arc that seemed endless. When they hit the ground, her head snapped back and rebounded from Jonathan's shoulder. He shouted with laughter, and she wanted to laugh with him, but the excitement of the ride had stolen her voice. She couldn't make a sound.

They glided to a stop, and her body went limp. His arms closed around her, and she fell back against his chest, content to let him hold her.

"I'm dizzy," she murmured. "So-o-o dizzy."

"Open your eyes, Paulette. Next time, keep them open. If you focus on a point in the distance, you won't lose your equilibrium."

His lips brushed her cheek and her eyes flew open. She kept them open while he kissed the side of her neck and the sensitive hollow at the angle of her jaw. She kept them open when he touched his mouth to hers, celebrating their conquest of the hill with a light, testing kiss that was over almost before it began.

But brief though it was, the contact was incendiary, and focusing on the distance didn't help Paulette keep her equilibrium. It didn't help at all.

Chapter Seven

Jonathan grinned at Paulette over the rim of his brandy snifter. "Want to know what I like about you?" he inquired.

Did she want to know? My God, wasn't it obvious? After the brazen way she had flirted with him, schemed and plotted to capture his attention and rearranged her social life to be with him, she was astonished he had to ask.

She licked a dollop of whipped cream off her finger and produced a luminous smile. "Do hogs like to wallow?"

She had abandoned the last scrap of subtlety, but it was worth it. Jonathan appeared to be suitably entranced. He sat back in the booth, resting his shoulders against the leather-padded partition as he said, "You're a good sport, that's what."

Was that all? He had been staring at her for the last fifteen minutes, ever since they'd arrived at the Laurel Tavern, and his display of interest had led her to believe he might say something more personal.

But maybe he was staring because her hair needed combing. Maybe she had whipped cream on her nose or lipstick on her teeth.

Come to think of it, an evening filled with chills and spills, with climbing hills and sledding down them couldn't be conducive to glamour. In their last run they'd parted company with the toboggan and landed in a heap. She had bumped her head, skinned her elbow, bruised her knee and wound up laughing till her sides ached at Jonathan's impersonation of Frosty the Snowman. But still she felt as if she'd been dragged over half the county by a runaway train and drop-kicked over the other half by the Green Bay Packers' punting team.

No doubt she should make a beeline for the ladies' room and make herself presentable. For the moment, however, the thought of leaving their cozy table for two was more than she could bear, so she sipped her Irish coffee and waited for Jonathan to go on.

"What I mean," he continued at last, "is that most of the women I know wouldn't have agreed to go tobogganing without a certain amount of coaxing—"

"Do you know a lot of women?"

"Don't change the subject, Paulette. Not when I'm in the middle of complimenting you on your lack of coyness. I like it that you didn't need coaxing. You were direct and spontaneous. You spoke your mind. You didn't play games. But what I find most refreshing is that you were able to forget your reservations and have a good time."

"Maybe I'm a masochist," she said. "But yes, I thought it was a fun evening."

"Yet you claim you're not athletic."

"I like to swim. I do a little yoga, but I'm not the outdoor type."

He glanced at the froth of whipped cream floating atop her drink. "You don't count calories either."

"Do you think I should?" She batted her lashes, and Jonathan chuckled at her pretense of modesty.

"Watch it, lady, or I'll have to take back what I said about coyness. You know damned well you have a fantastic figure."

"There are some things a woman never gets tired of hearing."

"So I've been told, but with all the men you know, you must hear it all the time."

"Not as often as you seem to think."

Jonathan's eyes narrowed. "Do you expect me to believe that?"

Paulette tried not to wince at the skepticism in his voice. "I expect you'll believe what you want to believe. And now it's my turn to ask you not to change the subject."

"I just wondered what your secret is—how you stay in shape."

"With due credit to my parents, I inherited a fast metabolism."

"Then you don't work out?"

"Not unless you count walking to and from the refrigerator." Paulette traced an elongated loop on the tabletop as she added, "I'm not a fitness freak, Jack. I'm not convinced there's any great virtue in sweating."

"But it's an accepted fact that regular exercise can be beneficial to your health."

"Accepted by whom? Hucksters who sell tennis rackets and running shoes?"

"The majority of doctors agrees, Paulette. You can't dispute the AMA."

"Why can't I? Diet and exercise aren't the only factors that influence longevity. There's genetics and environment and personality type and the kind of work we do. And most of all, there's stress. Which is why I choose to emphasize the quality of life and let quantity take care of itself."

Jonathan frowned as if she had confessed to some sort of heresy. "Isn't that a bit shortsighted? What if you knew that if you exercised half an hour a day you'd live to be eighty instead of seventy-five?"

"I'd probably learn to tap-dance, or I might start biking to work. But it's not that simple, is it?"

"Sure it is. Look at the statistics—"

"I'd rather not. Statistics are dehumanizing. They deal with probabilities and averages, but they don't tell you a thing about individuals."

"Point taken, but let's be realistic—"

"Please, Jack. After everything that's happened the last few weeks, reality's not my favorite thing."

Paulette expected Jonathan to belabor the issue, but he smiled and touched her cheek.

"Then we'll talk about something else," he said. "Choose a topic. Any topic."

"You," she answered softly. "Tell me about Jack Day."

He brushed a tendril of hair away from her brow. "I thought we'd gotten the bios out of the way last night."

"You told me your vital statistics, but that's only scratching the surface. Besides, you still owe me four questions."

"I wouldn't want to bore you."

"You won't, Jack. That's a promise."

He drew his thumb along the curve of her upper lip, turning her mouth up at the corners. "Go ahead. Ask your questions."

His reticence was intriguing. There were dozens of things she wanted to know about him. She wanted to know more about his family and his work and his fondness for fast cars. She wondered about the women in his life, and where he'd gotten his scarf.

The problem was finding an approach that would break through his reserve. But as luck would have it, she had faced similar problems at Shorewood. In her work for the undergraduate admissions committee she often interviewed prospective students, and she had developed techniques for drawing out the shyest of them.

"Tell me," she said, "if you could be anything you wanted, other than an investment counselor, what would you be?"

"That's a tough one," he replied. "Not that I always wanted to be a businessman, mind you. When I was a little kid I went through the usual cowboy, fireman, astronaut phases, and when I was in fifth grade, I wanted to play pro basketball."

He hesitated and she smiled, encouraging him to expand on his reply.

"You probably don't remember Wilt Chamberlain or Jerry West," he said.

"I remember Wilt the Stilt. Didn't he play for Los Angeles?"

"Among other teams," Jonathan qualified. "He and West were superstars, the Lakers' David and Goliath. God, they were something to see!"

"They were your heroes," Paulette remarked quietly.

"You might say that." Having admitted this much, Jonathan went on without prompting. "In junior high I was the tallest kid in my class—and the despair of the basketball coach. I was such a beanpole, my friends called me Skyhook. I shot up so fast, I couldn't cross the gym without bumping into the bleachers and tripping over my feet. But when I got to high school I actually made the varsity. Trouble was, I stopped growing at six-one. Of course, that's only two inches shorter than West, but he was one of a kind. A phenomenon, if you will. He had the kind of talent that overcame his height and made him a giant."

"So you're saying the career in business is your second choice."

"No, because one day toward the end of the tenth grade, while I was waiting for my brother to finish with the sports page, I started reading the financial section. There was an article about Charlie Smith, the guy who was head of Xerox, and it knocked me out. I mean, it was really fascinating. The next year, I signed up for Econ 1A, and for a class project I invested in some penny stocks. It was strictly a paper transaction, but it showed me I had a knack for picking winners, and from then on, I never looked back."

"And you've never regretted it?"

"No, never. Most people don't understand the kind of work I do. Either they see me as a glorified accountant, or they're afraid to take a chance. They see too many digits in front of the decimal point or they hear rumors of mergers or arbitrage or corporate raiders and they choke. Or maybe they get greedy. But no two ventures are the same. There's always a new challenge, always something new to learn."

"You were fortunate you discovered the direction you wanted to take when you were so young," Paulette murmured.

"I know I was," said Jonathan. "To be honest, I can't imagine doing anything else. But I believe in keeping my options open, so to get back to your question, I suppose if Wall Street were to shut down and I had to change my occupation, I'd become a sportscaster. Or maybe a carpenter. That's how my granddad started out. When I was in college I worked summers with one of his construction crews, and I liked working with wood—building things. There's something really satisfying about it."

Paulette nodded thoughtfully. "What gives you the greatest pleasure?"

"I hope I haven't tried it yet."

Jonathan replied in a lazy drawl that resonated along her nerve ends. He smiled into her eyes and a shock wave of longing washed through her.

"Next question," he said.

She cleared her throat, trying to regain her composure. "What do you want on your tombstone?"

Jonathan's eyebrows shot up. "Come again?"

"You heard me, Jack." She was pleased he looked startled. She had hoped to seize the offensive, but after faltering for a beat or two, he recovered.

"I'd rather be in Philadelphia," he declared.

"Beg pardon?"

"You heard me, Paulette. That's how I want my epitaph to read."

"I love it!" she cried. "You must be a W. C. Fields fan."

"Yep," said Jonathan. "I'm a sucker for slapstick."

"So am I. Laurel and Hardy. Harold Lloyd. The Marx Brothers—"

"How about the Three Stooges?"

"They were absolute geniuses! And Buster Keaton—"

"Oh, yeah. He was a riot with that sad, hound-dog face."

They exchanged nostalgic smiles, then Paulette folded her napkin and laid it next to her empty cup. "So, Jack, I gather I'm not the only one who's addicted to old movies."

Jonathan shrugged and signaled the barmaid for their check. "I've been known to watch the late show, Paulette. Not so much because of the movies as because it gives me an excuse to wallow in popcorn."

"Is that a fact?"

Another shrug was his only response.

"Well, don't look now, but your nose is growing."

He hemmed and hawed and protested a bit. He denied watching much commercial TV "except for news and sports." He said C-Span was his favorite channel. "Congressional hearings are more entertaining than soap operas," he insisted. "They have drama, humor, pathos, and they're *real*. Unlike you, Paulette, I find reality a turn-on."

But on the drive home, he confessed that he also watched *Wheel of Fortune*. "Doesn't everyone?" he inquired. He claimed the big attraction was Vanna White, and said, "She can dot my i's any old time."

Ungrateful wretch, thought Paulette. Here she was, indulging his yen to go tobogganing, ferrying him around town, trying to teach him the joys of Christmas, and he was drooling over a game-show hostess.

She stamped on the brakes and pulled up next to the curb, the better to glare at him.

He gave her a wolfish grin. "Do you know your eyes change color when you're angry? Even with the contacts—"

He reached out and turned the key in the ignition and her heart did a slow somersault. His arms slipped about her, and her breath lodged in her throat. His hands coasted along her spine, meeting above her shoulder blades to curve loosely about her neck. His thumbs lay along the wildly pounding pulses in her throat and held her so that she couldn't turn away. Even had she wanted to, there was no escaping the flurry of kisses that closed her eyes and sampled the winging arch of her brows and the sensitive lobe of one ear.

His mouth settled over her mouth with a tantalizing slowness, and of their own volition her arms crept upward to his shoulders, then twined about his neck. Her palms shaped themselves to the base of his skull, fingertips threading through crisp, dark hair, and her lips parted, inviting the sweet invasion of his tongue.

Jonathan wondered if she was thinking about Ben Gallagher. His hold on her tightened, and as one kiss blended into another the pressure of his mouth ranged from light and playful to rough and demanding.

But Paulette's mouth was just as urgent, her embrace as demanding as his. She felt his heart racing, heard his harsh intake of breath, and realized that from their first meeting she had been waiting for this moment, longing for Jonathan to kiss her like this, as if she were the only woman in the world for him. As if he were staking a claim.

But perhaps he was thinking of Vanna.

By the time he released her she was trembling inside. Only a fierce determination not to let him see how deeply he affected her steadied her hands as she started the car and eased away from the curb.

The remainder of the trip home was marked by silence. Paulette drove by rote, grateful that Jonathan didn't try to revive the conversation. Some things, she thought, were better left unsaid.

When they arrived at the apartment building, they managed the obligatory pleasantries. Paulette offered to help unload the toboggan, but Jonathan said he could handle it himself.

In light of the intimacies they had shared, he seemed strangely formal as he thanked her once more for the spruce tree. He told her he had enjoyed the evening, and she replied, "Thanks, Jack. So did I."

She bade him good-night and started along the walk, but when she reached the porch she turned for a last impulsive look at him. The same impulse made her inquire what he was doing Christmas Day.

"Without a car, I'm going to be stuck in Madison," she said, "and I thought, if you're not busy, we might spend the day together."

Jonathan lifted the toboggan off the roof of the Escort before he answered. "I'm surprised you don't have other plans."

Paulette had expected either a polite rejection or immediate acceptance. His noncommittal response made her uneasy. She leaned against the handrail, fingering the keys on her key chain as if they were worry beads as she replied, "The thing is, I'd intended to spend the holidays in Chicago with Annie Gallagher—"

"Any relation to Ben?"

"His wife. Or maybe I should say she's his bride. They've been married less than a month. But before the wedding, Anne and I made arrangements—"

"Let me get this straight," Jonathan persisted. "Are you telling me the Gallaghers are newlyweds?"

"That's right. They're just back from their honeymoon."

"And Anne Gallagher is your friend?"

"My closest friend," Paulette agreed. "She has been ever since she moved to Madison."

"Then why are you sneaking around with her husband?"

"Sneaking around?"

Jonathan stepped away from the car into a pool of moonlight. His expression was hard and purposeful as he strode toward the porch, and the rigid set of his shoulders expressed disapproval.

"I see what you're driving at," Paulette murmured. "Somehow you've gotten the idea that Ben's two-timing Anne, and I'm the third side of the triangle."

"Aren't you?"

"Heavens no! I've never heard anything more absurd! Ben's crazy about Annie, and even if he weren't, I would never do anything to hurt her."

"Then why'd you go out with him the other night?"

"I went out with *both* of them. Not that it's any of your business, but Ben asked me to help him choose Anne's Christmas present, so we went shopping and afterward we met Annie. There was no hanky-panky. I mean—good grief! What do you think I am?"

"Frankly, I don't know what to think." Jonathan propped the toboggan against the porch stairs, then looked at her and sighed. "You give off mixed signals, Paulette. I can't figure you out. You claim you have a reverence for tradition, but from the way you talk about marriage, your reverence doesn't extend that far—"

"Oh, I believe in marriage, all right. For *others*, not for me."

"There, you see! That's just what I'm talking about. One minute you're Mary Poppins, the next you're Sadie Thompson."

"Well, whoever I am, I'm not the sort of woman who betrays her friends."

"Then you have my apologies. I misread the situation and I'm sorry about that. But I won't apologize for misjudging you. Not when you've gone to such lengths to cloud the issue. You pretend to be direct and open, to say what's on your mind, but it's all an act. I can't decide if you're a fraud or scared to death."

"Don't be silly. What would I be scared of?"

"I couldn't begin to guess. Commitment, maybe. Losing your freedom." Jonathan slouched against the newel post, arms folded across his chest. "There's one thing I do know," he added. "You can't come on like a swinger, then take offense when your performance convinces me you are one."

"Can't I? Just watch me, Jack Day."

Paulette replied in a small, cold voice, scarcely above a whisper. But the mutinous tilt of her chin as she opened the street door and flounced into the vestibule conveyed her outrage.

Jonathan caught the door before it slammed and followed her inside. He waited until she had climbed the stairs and let herself into the studio, then, with a weary shake of his head, he went into his own apartment.

It seemed there was nothing more he could say. No doubt he had already said too much.

He understood Paulette's anger. If their positions were reversed and she had told him some unpleasant truths about himself, he'd be angry too. But pride made him feel he had been right not to apologize.

Why should he blame himself for their falling out? Was it his fault Paulette changed images as often as he changed socks?

His common sense said "No," but his conscience answered with a stern unequivocal "Yes."

Despite her inconsistencies, whether she was the jaded sophisticate adding new definitions to his lexicon of *fun* or the pink-cheeked ingenue stringing popcorn for his tree, one aspect of Paulette remained constant. There was a hint of vulnerability about her, rarely glimpsed and quickly hidden by a mask of cool indifference. But those brief glimpses were enough to make him wonder how much of her exterior was a sham.

Was she as confident as she seemed or was her flippancy a defense mechanism? And if it was a defense mechanism, what was she concealing? Somewhere inside, was part of her still that forlorn little girl who had yearned for Chatty Cathy and believed in Santa Claus? Was she clinging to her dreams, dreading disillusion?

Jonathan took off his jacket and scarf while he considered these possibilities. He pulled off his boots and stretched out on the sofa, and gradually he became aware of Paulette moving about the studio.

Hands behind his head, he stared at the ceiling, distracted by her almost soundless pacing. From the swaying of the chandelier and the intermittent gurgle of water through the pipes, she must be walking a circuitous route from the kitchen to the main room. His eyes smarted as he followed her footsteps back and forth, to and fro, a dozen times or more.

What the devil was she doing up there? Why did she keep turning the tap on and off? Didn't she realize it was past 2:00 a.m.? She had the day off; she could sleep late. But he didn't have that luxury. Why didn't she knock it off and go to bed? For that matter, why didn't he? If he fell asleep on the couch, he'd wake up with a crick in his neck. It happened every time— He growled an oath, and as if Paulette had heard him, silence descended on the studio.

"Finally," Jonathan muttered.

He dragged himself to his feet and switched off the living-room lights. He unzipped his ski bib on the way to the bedroom and stripped to his briefs in the darkness, letting his clothes fall where they might. He was yawning as he got into bed, but the moment his head touched the pillow, he heard Paulette's shower running.

It shouldn't have bothered him. Under ordinary circumstances he would hardly have noticed the sound. But the events of the last few days were far from ordinary. He had met Paulette and kissed her. An hour ago he had held her in his arms.

If he had known then that she was not having an affair with Ben Gallagher, would he have let her go?

He had no ready answer to this question, and he rolled onto his back and lay spread-eagled, listening to the muffled rush of water.

When he closed his eyes, he could see Paulette standing in her shower. He envisioned her lifting her arms and turning her face to the spray, like a flower stretching toward the sun. He saw her hair darken from copper to auburn to chestnut brown as it absorbed the water; saw it so clearly that he could feel its heavy tug at the fragile stem of her neck.

And then he saw the rest of her—slender, rounded, exquisitely formed, her skin dewy and flushed from the heat of the water.

He charted the course of a single droplet from the moment of its inception in her sleek dark mane until it fell of its own accord to her shoulder, then trickled along her collarbone to converge with the rivulet in the valley between her breasts. He watched the droplet separate itself from the rest of the stream and meander across her bosom, lingering when it reached the blush-pink crest as if it could not bear to leave its purchase. The droplet clung there, crystalline and pure, until a fresh cascade dislodged it and it rushed on, flowing over the curves and hollows of belly and hips and thighs, searching out the secrets of her body.

Jonathan groaned and punched his pillow. He cursed his overactive imagination, but could not stop the images.

He watched Paulette reach for a cake of soap, his vision so detailed that he knew the soap was white and smooth and slippery, as slippery as her skin. He saw the languid movements of her hands as she worked up a lather, and the fragrance of violets surrounded him as she smoothed the lather over her face, her throat, her arms— Suddenly his perspective shifted. He was with her in the shower, and although he was standing behind her, she sensed his presence. She glanced at him and smiled, offering him the soap. Then she raised her hands, and with a fluid, seductive grace swept her hair to the top of her head, inviting him to wash her back.

He felt awkward, all thumbs; aware of her delicacy and aroused by it, yet protective. His hands felt huge and powerful as they moved over her, tracing random patterns through the foam, molding themselves to her splendors. Everywhere he touched her she was soft and wet and receptive, warm and womanly, and the feel of her water-slicked skin drove thoughts of gentleness from his mind.

He wound his arms about her and folded her close, capturing her breasts in the curved bowls of his palms.

His thumbs feathered over the pouting areolas, coaxing the nipples into tightly budded peaks, and her head lolled to one side, as if she could not support its weight.

She arched across his forearm, yielding herself to him, and he bent over her and buried his face in her bosom. He wanted to immerse himself in her softness, but for now he was content to cover her breasts with small biting kisses. He tongued her nipples, then trapped one between his teeth. It filled his mouth with the taste of violets and his body with an overwhelming need to possess her. To be possessed by her.

He dropped to his knees, then eased backward into a corner of the stall until he was half reclining, drawing her after him so that she was seated astride his thighs. His fingers braceleted her ankles and left soapy designs on her calves as he wrapped her legs about his hips.

"Not yet," she whispered, and bending over him, she freed her hands and indicated that he should lie back. "It's your turn," she whispered.

He watched, entranced by her shy sensuality, while she applied the soap to his shoulders and chest, while her hands slipped over him in ever-widening circles. Slowly. So slowly.

He was desperate for her. He thought he would die if he had to wait much longer, and he put his hands over hers to guide them, and while her caresses moved lower, she leaned forward and pressed her mouth to his.

Ah, God! She was heaven.

He positioned himself and felt her opening to him, enveloping him— The shower stopped. Reality intruded. He was alone in his room, aching and unfulfilled.

"Dammit!"

He hurled his pillow at the windows, vaulted out of bed and staggered toward the bathroom. He stubbed his toe against the door on his way to the hall, and he was still muttering curses while he adjusted the taps for his own shower.

The water was lukewarm at best, and he realized Paulette must have used all the hot. But that was all right. Just now he needed a reminder that tonight he'd gotten off easily.

If he saw much more of Paulette, the future might hold dangers more devastating than stubbed toes and cold showers.

Chapter Eight

Jonathan knew the risks. He had only imagined the pleasures. Yet when his alarm went off the following morning, his first thought was that he had to see Paulette.

He heard her phone ring while he was shaving. The promptness with which she answered the call made him wonder if she had slept as badly as he had.

He skipped his morning workout and made some instant coffee. He drank it standing at the kitchen counter, trying to rouse himself from his inertia. He was debating whether to have a second cup when he recalled Paulette's suggestion that they celebrate Christmas together.

"I thought if you're not busy, we might spend the day together," she'd said.

The fly in the ointment was, he had reservations that evening for a flight to Seattle. Until last weekend he had looked forward to the trip. No matter where he traveled or what he was doing the other fifty-one weeks of the year, he had never missed a Christmas at home, and that included the year Jocelyn had married his brother. To him, and to the rest of the Days, Christmas and family were inseparable; a time to forget about rivalries and close ranks.

But now that he had discovered Paulette was not romantically involved with Ben Gallagher, the thought of Christmas in Seattle seemed less appealing.

On the spur of the moment, he got Paulette's number from directory assistance and tried it. Her line was busy, so he decided to stop by the studio before he left for work.

He had to knock several times before she opened the door, tousled and sleepy-eyed, wrapped in a yellow quilted robe. She looked younger without makeup, smaller without her shoes, and without the contacts her eyes were soft and unfocused, a gentle gray-green.

He smiled. She didn't, but neither did she frown. After a slight hesitation, she waved him inside.

"Be right with you," she said. "I'm on the phone."

He was relieved that she didn't seem to harbor any grudges, and he realized belatedly that the living room had been transformed. Red poinsettias banked the windows; white ones skirted the tree. Pink azaleas gave an incandescent brightness to the corners of the room and bracketed the lawn chairs.

The profusion of flowerpots solved one mystery: In all her to-ing and fro-ing and turning the tap on and off last night, Paulette must have been watering the plants.

But where had they come from?

While she was in the kitchen finishing her phone call, Jonathan wandered about the living area, stealing glances at the cards attached to the plants. The signatures confirmed his suspicions. Curtis and Scott and Phillip—men one and all.

Some guy named Richard had sent a variety of plants, along with his undying devotion. One of his messages, tucked among the blooms of a flame-colored cyclamen, read, "I miss you, my darling. Won't you give me another chance?"

"Sorry to keep you waiting, Jack."

Paulette's apology made him jump. He stepped away from the cyclamen and tried to appear nonchalant. With a brusque jut of his chin toward the poinsettias, he observed, "That's quite a haul. The place looks like a greenhouse."

"They are a bit much," Paulette allowed. "Not that I don't appreciate the sentiment."

"They're from your boyfriends?"

Paulette eyed him soberly, puzzled by his flat, insinuating tone. "You're half right. The plants are from friends, but they're men, not boys."

"Not very imaginative, are they?"

"In what way?"

Jonathan thrust his hands into his pockets and appeared to be studying the toes of his shoes. If she didn't know better, she'd think he was embarrassed. She gave him time to explain, but after a minute had passed he looked so uncomfortable that she took pity on him.

"The plants are lovely," she said. "I just wish I had room for them all."

"Does that mean you're not keeping them?"

"Not all of them, no."

"What'll you do with 'em?"

"If I can arrange to return the Escort this afternoon instead of this morning, what I'd like to do is keep one or two of the poinsettias and distribute the rest to nursing homes."

"Well, if it turns out you can't keep the Escort, I'll help deliver the plants."

"In your car?"

"You have my word I won't exceed the speed limit."

Paulette's smile made him feel as if the sun had broken through storm clouds. "In that case, it's a deal."

"Great! I'll see you later then."

"Later," she echoed, following him to the hall. "Before you leave, aren't you going to tell me why you came by?"

"Of course." He clapped his palm to his forehead. "Stupid of me to forget. The thing is, I got to wondering if your invitation for tomorrow was still open?"

"What if it is?"

He braced himself against the banister and met her gaze. "I'd like to take you up on it."

"All right! You've got yourself a date for Christmas dinner, Jack. I'll bring the turkey—"

"And I'll bring the mistletoe."

With a grin that took her breath away, Jonathan did an about-face and sprinted down the stairs.

THE PHONE RANG CONSTANTLY that morning, and the calls made Paulette fall behind schedule. She was half an hour late returning the Escort to the dealership, and to save time, she took a taxi home.

Nicole phoned just before noon. By the time Paulette finished talking with her sister, the day had lost its glow. She wanted to be upbeat and supportive, but Nicole's track record didn't leave much room for optimism.

What could you say to a woman whose marital history sounded like a soap opera?

At eighteen, while vacationing with a classmate in California, Nicole had met Simon Avery, a man three times her age who had made her his bride, and shortly before their first anniversary, a very wealthy widow.

Seven months after Simon's death, Nicole gave birth to his daughter, and not quite a year later she married Clayton Avery.

Clayton was Simon's eldest son, which technically speaking made Nicole her own mother-in-law. He was closer to Nicole's age than his father had been, but he was a perennial Peter Pan. In many ways, though, they were an ideal match, as happy and carefree as children playing house. Then Clayton found another playmate, and at twenty-four Nicole found herself older but not appreciably wiser, five months pregnant and newly divorced.

At first it appeared she had learned from her mistakes. After her son was born she told Paulette, "When I met Simon I was looking for security and I got a bonus. No one ever loved me the way Simon did. Probably no one ever will. For as long as he lived I had position, respect, a sense of identity—But there weren't many fireworks between us. So with Clayton I was looking for passion, and he tried to give it to me. God knows, we both tried to make it work. But then he began to have problems—You know. In the bedroom. He said when he was with me, he felt inadequate. Now I'm a two-time loser, and I'm going to quit while I'm ahead. I've got my looks and my health and my children, and I don't have to worry about money. I don't need a man to give my life meaning. All I need is time to find myself."

Nicole started seeing an analyst to help her in her search, and six months later, she married him.

"Knowledge," she told Paulette. "That's what life's all about. We're put on this earth to learn, to acquire wisdom, and Tony's the most intelligent man I've ever met."

Anthony Halliday was intelligent, there was no question about that. He had a soaring IQ, a thriving practice, an income to match, and charm enough for two. He was the right age for Nicole, he was fond of her children and devoted to her. She sang his praises. "We're compatible in every way," she told Paulette.

But after a year of wedlock, Nicole changed her tune. The first sign of trouble came as a postscript in one of her infrequent letters.

"Never marry a doctor," she wrote. "I saw more of Tony when I was his patient than I do as his wife."

Over the next few months Nicole lost sight of her husband's virtues. She felt neglected, and as her litany of complaints grew, she drifted into a string of infidelities.

"There are times when experience is a fair substitute for wisdom," she wrote. "I've learned that other men appreciate me, even if Tony does not."

The marriage limped along for another year, until Nicole's liaison with the masseur at her health club became a matter of public knowledge. In July she had written, "Eddie's gorgeous. He's perfect—like a young Adonis." He was also, Nicole confessed, barely twenty-one.

In September, Tony filed for divorce. To protect her interests, Nicole filed a countersuit, and for the past three months, their efforts to work out a property settlement had thrown them together.

"It's ironic," Nicole told Paulette on this December 24. "If I'd seen this much of Tony before he walked out, we might never have separated."

"Is there any possibility of a reconciliation?" Paulette asked.

"None whatsoever. Tony had his chance and he blew it. I've got Eddie now."

"You're still seeing him?"

"As often as I can. He's an incredible man, Paulette."

What Paulette found incredible was that Nicole hadn't told their parents about the divorce.

"Tell them," she urged her sister.

"I will," said Nicole. "Eventually."

Nicole's *eventuallys* had a nasty habit of turning into *nevers*. "Waiting's not going to make it any easier," Paulette cautioned. "What if Mother and Dad find out from someone else?"

"I almost wish they would." A wheedling note crept into Nicole's voice as she added, "I don't suppose you'd be willing to break the news."

Paulette said no, she wouldn't, and asked about her niece and nephew.

"They're fine," Nicole replied shortly. Even long-distance from San Francisco, Paulette could tell that her sister was sulking.

It's her nickel, Paulette reminded herself, *and the divorce is her problem, not mine.*

"Nicole's your sister," an inner voice argued. "If she can't muster the courage to put your parents in the picture, perhaps you should take it upon yourself to fill them in."

That wouldn't be doing Nicole any favors, thought Paulette. *She needs to confront them herself.*

"But what if they do hear about the divorce from someone else? It could happen. Tony might tell them. One of the children might let something slip. Think how hurt they'd be."

They'll be hurt in any case, and this is not the sort of news Mother and Dad would relish hearing from me.

"You're damned if you do and damned if you don't," the inner voice agreed, "so why not get it over with?"

Duty was not high on Paulette's hit parade. There were occasions, however, when obligations could not be ignored. This, she realized, was one of them.

If only she knew where her duty lay.

An hour after Nicole's call ended, still fretting about duty, Paulette had made a molded cranberry salad and mixed filling for the pumpkin pies. The pies were in the oven before it dawned on her that she should simply let matters ride.

Christmas Eve, she decided, was no time to be the bearer of bad tidings.

But before the afternoon was over, she had to phone her parents, and she dreaded making the call. Her mother had an uncanny knack for ferreting out secrets, and she was particularly tenacious when the secrets concerned one of her daughters.

Paulette's only recourse was to steer the conversation away from Nicole. *And pray for a miracle,* she thought.

Her father answered the phone in his booming parson's voice, but as they talked about the weather, her job, his parishioners, he sounded vague and somewhat distant, as if his thoughts were engaged with weightier matters.

Finally, he said, "Your mother wants to speak to you. Let me put her on."

"Paulette? How are you?"

"Fine, Mother. Never better. And you?"

A feeling of loneliness engulfed Paulette as she listened to her mother's response. She wished she could confide in her parents. "Dad must be working on a sermon," she said.

"Yes, dear. His homily for tonight."

Paulette smiled and pictured her father pacing about his study, trying out phrases and gesturing at the walls, his reading glasses perched on top of his head.

"When are you coming to see us?" her mother inquired.

"Probably not till spring break. I've had to take quite a bit of time off lately, with the fire and all. But why don't you and Dad come to Madison?"

"We'd love to, dear, but I don't see how we can get away."

"Not even for a couple of days?"

"No, not even that. You know how your father is. He's never been able to delegate responsibility."

"Neither have you, Mother."

"That's true. Much as I'd like a vacation, we never seem to manage one."

That's the trouble with being indispensable, Paulette thought, but she didn't say it out loud.

"Did you get the packages we sent, Paulette?"

"Yes, they're here, under the tree."

"You haven't opened them?"

"No, Mother. I haven't even peeked."

"Promise you won't. Not till tomorrow."

Paulette promised she would save her presents till morning. She swore that she was eating properly, getting enough sleep, staying out of drafts.

"Stop worrying, Mother," she said. "I'm a big girl now."

"Of course you are, dear. Believe me, I don't mean to nag, but I can't help worrying. I hate to think of you spending Christmas alone."

"Well, you can put your mind at ease. I won't be alone. I'm fixing dinner for my landlord."

There was a brief silence, and then her mother said, "I didn't know you could cook."

"I'm quite capable in the kitchen," said Paulette. "Not that I could compete with you, but you'll be pleased to hear I'm using your recipe for the stuffing."

"My gracious! I'm more than pleased. I'm flattered."

Good, thought Paulette. I hoped you would be. And before her mother could quiz her about Jonathan, Paulette said goodbye.

JONATHAN MADE A FEW phone calls of his own that afternoon. He had reservations to cancel; a new flight to arrange.

It took some doing to switch his airline tickets to Monday. He listened to Muzak until his ears were numb. He dealt with one agent who informed him at least six times that this was the busiest season of the year, and another who thought she was God. He had to give up a direct flight to Seattle-Tacoma and travel by way of St. Louis, and when all that was accomplished, he had to phone Seattle and tell his parents about the change in plans.

Jocelyn took his call. "Everyone else is at work, Jonny. Have you forgotten about the time difference?"

Jonathan waited for the familiar pangs of loss to grip him, but nothing happened. Nary a twinge. Jocelyn's breathy, little-girl voice left him curiously unmoved.

"I haven't forgotten," he replied, "but before Mom and Dad leave for the airport, I wanted to tell them not to expect me."

"You're not coming?"

"Not till next week."

"You've never missed a family Christmas before, Jonny."

"No, this'll be a first."

"Does it have anything to do with me?"

"No, Jocelyn. The postponement has no connection with you."

"We'll miss you, Jonny. *I'll* miss you."

There'd been a time not so very long ago when he would have given his right arm to hear Jocelyn admit that she thought about him at all. Now all he felt was a kind of benign annoyance.

He stood at his office window, looking down at Capitol Square, watching the traffic lights on the corner of Mifflin Street change from red to green. Dusk was settling over the city. A fine, powdery snow had started to fall, but despite the limited visibility, he felt as if he had never seen things more clearly.

He tried to recall why he had ever fancied himself in love with Jocelyn. He remembered that he had once been captivated by her corn silk hair and prom queen prettiness, but for the life of him, he couldn't bring her face into focus.

Instead of long flaxen hair he saw a cap of marigold curls; instead of blue eyes, he saw eyes that were haunting smoky-green—

"Jonny? Are you still there?"

The husky catch in Jocelyn's voice made him feel uneasy. He wished she wouldn't call him Jonny, especially in that intimate, caressing tone. She was his brother's wife, for God's sake! And although there were times when Larry could be a pain in the neck, if push came to shove, there was no question where his loyalty would lie—and it wouldn't be with his sister-in-law.

"Jonny? Can you hear me?"

"Yes, Jocelyn, I hear you."

"Did you hear me say I'll miss you?"

"I'll miss you, too," he answered heartily. "I'll miss the whole family. But it can't be helped. Something came up at the last minute."

HE LEFT THE OFFICE in time to make several purchases, and when he got home, Paulette was hanging a wreath on the street door.

"What do you think?" she called as he pulled into the driveway.

"Looks good." He removed a shopping bag from the passenger seat and approached her along the walk. "Just a little crooked," he added.

"So was the kid I bought it from." She moved into the twilight, a few feet away from the door, and turned to assess the lopsided arrangement of pine boughs and ribbons. "Ah, well," she sighed. "It was for a good cause. If this were a perfect world, all the Boy Scouts would be Beaver Cleaver, the parents would be Ward and June, and the daughters would be Mary Richards."

Jonathan put his hand on her shoulder and she glanced up at him.

"I was teasing, Paulette."

"So was I," she said. But her smile seemed forced.

Snowflakes glistened in her hair. One had landed at the corner of her mouth.

Lucky snowflake, he thought, and followed her inside.

Chapter Nine

Jonathan was in the mood for an evening at home. At intervals throughout the day he had entertained visions of candlelight, supper by the fireside and Paulette in his arms.

He hadn't forgotten his offer to help with the poinsettias, but he'd had too many things on his mind to worry about the plants. If he thought about them at all, he minimized the task of getting rid of them.

After all, how long could it take to deliver a few poinsettias to nursing homes? An hour, perhaps an hour and a half tops. Right?

Wrong.

To begin with, since morning Paulette had received more plants—three of them from Richard. She had moved the overflow into the vestibule, along with enough baskets of fruit and boxes of candy to stock a grocery store.

In the second place, there was not a lot of room in his car.

The Cobra had been built for style and speed. It was great for zipping in and out of traffic, even better on steep mountain roads, and it was at its best gobbling up miles on the highway.

His car was also a status symbol. It projected the image of a man accustomed to power; a man on his way to the top. It said he was not afraid to take chances, and that he would overcome any obstacle to achieve his goal.

Jocelyn thought the car was sexy, and she was not alone. The Cobra usually impressed impressionable females. It made him the envy of other men—most notably, his brother—but it was not designed to haul freight.

The driver and one passenger could ride in relative comfort if both of them traveled light. Once he and Paulette were in their seats, there wasn't much space for poinsettias, which meant that they had to make more trips than he had anticipated.

Another thing he hadn't counted on was that Paulette would want to visit with the old folks. He had assumed they would drop off some plants and maybe a basket of fruit, extend season's greetings to the staff and patients, and be on their way. He figured ten minutes was the most each stop would take.

Wrong again.

At Lakeview Nursing Home he made the mistake of waiting at the front desk while Paulette went off to say hello to the residents.

"Back in a jiffy," she said.

She was gone half an hour, during which he cooled his heels and brooded about all those poinsettias—and the men who had given them to her.

They were friends, she'd said, but were they her lovers as well? And if they were, how many had she had affairs with? Two or three? More than a few? All of them?

Was she seeing anyone now?

He wanted to ask, but couldn't find the nerve. If Paulette told him she was seeing someone else, where would that leave him?

At Elderhouse they were invited to watch a Christmas pageant. At Sunset Ridge they joined a group of carolers and fa-la-la'ed their way through the wards. At Oakwood they had cookies and punch, and at Orchard Manor, their last stop, a pair of wizened old gentlemen in wheelchairs attached themselves to Paulette.

"Lookee what Santa brought!" one of them cackled. He tried to pinch Paulette's bottom, but she managed to elude him.

"Mind your manners, Henry," codger number two scolded. "You're acting like a lecherous old goat."

"Damned right, and proud of it," Henry replied, unrepentant. "It's a darned sight more fun than droppin' money at the mall and watchin' the young girls bend over to pick it up."

When they left the nursing home, Henry chased Paulette along the corridor to the main entrance, the tires on his wheelchair squealing against the tile floor.

"Hey, toots," he wheezed. "Wanna come to my room and cuddle?"

"Not tonight," Paulette replied. "I'm here with another fella."

"Then how 'bout a kiss?"

She smiled and gently kissed his bald pate and told him she'd see him soon. In the Cobra, as Jonathan drove homeward, she said, "That's what I like about old people. You don't have to wonder where you stand with them. They've stopped pretending."

"They can afford to," Jonathan answered gruffly, wondering where he stood with her. "If a younger man pulled the kind of pranks Henry pulls, he'd get arrested."

It was after nine-thirty, and the streets were nearly deserted. Reflex made Jonathan accelerate, but the instant the car picked up speed, Paulette reminded him of his promise.

"Sorry," he muttered.

A scowl knotted his forehead. He felt a headache gathering at the back of his skull. *Too many unanswered questions,* he thought.

At the apartment building, they piled out of the car and started along the walk.

"Hey, toots," he called. "Wanna come to my room and cuddle?"

Paulette's smile said she didn't take him seriously. "Not enough time," she replied.

"Why? Do you turn into a pumpkin at ten?"

"I thought we might go to midnight mass."

"Then how about some food?" Jonathan suggested. "I'm starving."

He warmed up some mushroom soup and crisped rashers of bacon while she made toast and sliced tomatoes for sandwiches. They ate by candlelight because he owed it to himself to make at least one aspect of his vision a reality, and afterward they got into their coats and walked the few blocks to St. Andrew's on Regent Street.

THE SMALL STONE CHURCH was redolent with the fragrance of greens, spiced with incense and candle wax, washed in a hazy golden light. An usher greeted them at the door and showed them to seats in the back pew just as a trumpet fanfare sounded the opening of a Bach prelude. The organ joined the trumpet in a soaring arpeggio that sent chills down Jonathan's spine.

The priest appeared, stately and serene, his crisp, snowy vestments crackling with gold embroidery. He followed the cross and his column of acolytes down the aisle, and just as the procession passed, another couple squeezed into the pew. As they rose to their feet, Jonathan moved closer to Paulette. Her hair brushed his chin when she turned to share the hymnal, and his concentration was shattered.

He knelt for prayers and read the responses. He stood beside her for another hymn. He sat on the bench and tried to focus on the lesson, but how could he pay attention to the Scriptures when Paulette was so near?

The pew was crowded. They were wedged in their places like sardines in a can, yet he hardly noticed the woman on his left.

Paulette filled his senses. He was acutely aware of her knee grazing his trouser leg, her thigh snug against his. Her scent was more fragrant than incense, the delicate line of her profile more compelling than the sermon. When their fingers met on the smooth, dark binding of the hymnal, her touch was a benediction.

Even when they were kneeling at the communion rail, he couldn't stop looking at her. Thinking about her. Exulting in her nearness.

It should have seemed sacrilegious. He realized that. But his feelings were not irreverent. They seemed a part of the ritual; a blend of physical passion and love.

Love?

The moment this idea popped into his mind, Jonathan retreated from it. Part of him—the rational part—said that love required intimacy, sharing, *time*. And since he had met Paulette only last Monday, what he felt for her couldn't possibly be love.

He must be confusing desire with adoration, a yearning for some adolescent ideal. He wasn't certain the Paulette he thought he knew existed. She might be a product of his overactive imagination.

And yet, the romantic in him wondered, what if she did exist? What if the attraction went beyond infatuation? What if she felt the same way about him? Wouldn't he be wise to stop analyzing his feelings before he destroyed them?

The service ended on the stroke of midnight. Church bells pealed while the congregation filed out of the pews.

Paulette introduced him to the minister, and Father Walsh offered Jonathan a toothy smile and a firm handshake, but his eyes never strayed from Paulette.

"I'm surprised to see you here tonight," he said. "I thought you'd be in Minneapolis with your parents."

"Not this year, Father. I—it's too complicated to explain."

The priest combed his fingers through his shock of white hair. His smile cooled a bit. "Your parents are well, I trust."

"Yes, Father. Busy as ever."

"And your sister?"

"Nicole is—Nicole."

"Is she still living in Los Angeles?"

"San Francisco," Paulette answered, and before Father Walsh could inquire about Nicole's husband, she gave Jonathan's coat sleeve a beseeching tug.

"I guess we should be going," he said.

"Yes, we should." Already edging away from the priest, Paulette said, "Another engagement, Father. You understand."

Jonathan felt the minister's puzzled gaze following him as he hurried after Paulette.

"Why the rush?" he asked, but she didn't answer. She was dodging through the crowd, straining against his hand. She broke into a trot, and he lengthened his stride to keep pace with her.

The snow had thickened while they were in church. It eddied about them in lacy gusts that shrouded the landscape and dusted their hair and shoulders. Paulette didn't slow down until St. Andrew's had vanished in the snow; they were crossing Van Hise Street before she spoke again.

"I suppose I owe you an explanation," she said.

"Take your time," he replied. "Make it a good one."

She ducked her head and trudged along beside him, watching the soles of her boots sink into the drifted snow near the curb.

"Would you settle for the truth?"

"Try me."

"The truth is, my sister has separated from her husband, and she hasn't told my parents. I'd rather they didn't hear the news from a third party."

"Are you afraid the pastor would tell them?"

"No, not intentionally. But I can't take the chance. Unless I wanted to lie to him, it seemed safer to get out of there."

"Commendable," said Jonathan. "Too bad you had to lie about the late date."

"But I didn't lie. Not exactly. What I told Father Walsh was that we had other plans, so the most I'm guilty of is telling a fib." She tilted her head to one side and looked up at him. "I kind of hoped you'd suggest something that would make it come true."

Jonathan grinned and tucked her hand through his arm. "Play your cards right and that might be arranged."

"Thanks, Jack. I knew I could count on you."

She moved closer to him, rubbed her cheek against his shoulder, and with that inspiration he had no shortage of ideas. It was too late for a leisurely supper, but it wasn't too late for dessert. And he knew precisely what he wanted that dessert to be.

Within a quarter-hour of their arrival at his apartment, birch logs blazed in the fireplace. Candlelight shimmered on the ceiling. The minilights on the spruce tree flickered red and blue and green. An album spun on the turntable, and the poignant lyricism of Winton Marsalis's trumpet wove a lush tapestry of sound in the room.

Jonathan took off his jacket and tie and dropped them on the sofa along with Paulette's coat. He tossed some pillows near the hearth and invited her to make herself comfortable, then excused himself and went into the kitchen.

She took him at his word and sat on one of the pillows to remove her boots. Her feet were icy, her toes half frozen. She massaged them briskly, and they were pink and tingling when she heard the pop of a champagne cork.

She heard the clink of glassware, the slam of the refrigerator door, and when Jonathan returned to the living room, carrying a tray laden with chilled champagne, a pair of long-stemmed goblets and a wedge of brie ringed by crackers, he found her lounging among the cushions, warming her feet by the fire.

"This is lovely," she murmured.

So are you, he thought.

Bathed in firelight and the glow of candles, she looked flushed and rosy, soft and sensuous; utterly delectable and completely irresistible.

For long breathless moments he stood gazing down at her. The fire at his back accentuated his size. She saw him in silhouette, and her perspective gave her a keen awareness of his height, of the rugged width of his shoulders beneath his white oxford cloth shirt, the breadth of his chest, his long sloping flanks.

She sensed his urgency, the immediacy of his need, and knew that she must make a choice: Leave now or stay the night.

His intentions were clear; she was not at all sure they coincided with hers, yet she couldn't seem to move.

Her apartment would be cold and empty, and Jonathan's big, rangy body offered warmth and comfort, an escape from loneliness.

"I forgot the mistletoe," he confessed, his voice rough with emotion.

"That's all right. We don't really need it, do we?"

He smiled and sat down on a cushion facing her. "Merry Christmas, Paulette."

She raised her glass, repeated the toast and drank it. As he refilled her glass, a log settled on the grate. Flames leaped up, etching his features a ruddy bronze, and through some strange alchemy of wine and music he seemed to radiate heat and light.

It might have been an optical illusion, a capricious trick of the light, but she took it as an omen. In that magical instant she realized how much she wanted him, and when he stretched out beside her and opened his arms, she went into them.

She wanted to make love with him, but she refused to romanticize her feelings.

Love was a pipe dream for poets and paperback novels. It was fine for old Doris Day movies and for lovable people like Anne and Ben, and maybe, once upon a time, for her parents. But she had stopped expecting to be loved about the same time she'd stopped believing in Santa Claus, and she got along without love very well, thank you.

All she wanted was for Jonathan to hold her close. She wanted to be part of him—to make him part of herself. *Just for tonight,* she thought.

Then he kissed her, and she couldn't think at all.

Chapter Ten

"Oscar Wilde once said, 'The only way to get rid of temptation is to yield to it.'"

"Oscar," said Jonathan, "didn't know you."

Paulette thumbed her nose at him and reached for another chocolate-covered cherry, but as she popped the candy into her mouth, she acknowledged the element of truth in Jonathan's observation.

She couldn't resist chocolate-covered cherries any more than she could resist him.

It was Sunday evening. They had been together since Thursday night, but her longing for him hadn't diminished. Quite the contrary. Every time they made love her excitement fed upon itself and grew stronger, more consuming.

Since Christmas Eve they had shared meals and confidences, talk and laughter, and a few memorable silences. They had slept together, wakened to passion, and slept again. She had listened to music with Jonathan, and lived out a fantasy or two with him in his king-size tub. She'd argued politics with him, bluffed her way through a chess match with him, and read the comic strips with him.

She had introduced him to *Doonesbury*, and he had introduced her to sensual pleasures she hadn't known existed—hadn't even suspected.

He was a considerate lover; gentle and passionate, inventive and tireless, endlessly demanding yet endlessly patient; as concerned with her needs as with his own. And she would do almost anything he asked of her. Happily. Scrub his back, make his coffee, warm his bed, admire his car— She'd stopped answering her phone, had even given up this year's telecast of *It's a Wonderful Life* so that he could watch the Lakers' game.

But there was one thing she wouldn't do.

She watched him going through his calisthenics, enjoying the sinuous play of muscles in his thighs and buttocks as he limbered up for his run.

He hadn't been jogging since Tuesday, and he missed his daily workout. He'd gotten out of bed this morning feeling keyed-up, restive. After breakfast he'd said, "I need some exercise. It helps my disposition."

"I don't know about yours," she'd replied, watching him prowl for the dozenth time from the fireplace to the bay windows, "but if you'd go jogging, it would certainly help mine."

Since noon he had been pestering her to go out with him, and she had steadfastly refused.

His warm-up completed, Jonathan hitched up his crew socks and tightened the laces on his Nikes.

"Sure you won't change your mind?" he asked.

"Positive." She smiled because he seemed more cheerful already, and riffled the pages of the *TV Guide*. "There's a Jimmy Cagney movie I want to see."

Jonathan pulled on the insulated Lakers jacket she'd given him for Christmas and pronounced it a perfect fit.

But instead of leaving he propped his hands on the sofa back, trapping her between his arms as he lowered his torso in a modified push-up. Then, supporting his weight on the tripod of his toes and fingertips, he rocked forward until his forehead rested against hers.

"You don't know what you're missing, Paulette."

"D'you mean frostbite?" She gave a mock shiver. "It's ten degrees out there."

"Once you get going, you won't notice the cold."

"I'd notice," she said.

"But it's worth it," he insisted. "Jogging's a great conditioner. You should try it at least once."

She shook her head slowly, so that their noses rubbed.

"Please," he whispered against her lips. "As a favor to me."

She felt herself weakening and broke the kiss before it could become deeper, more persuasive.

"No," she declared. "Not even for you, Jack."

Jonathan levered himself a fraction of an inch lower, renewing the kiss with an open-mouthed ardor that made her senses reel, and when her resistance reached its nadir, he asked, "Is that your final decision?"

"It is, and it's not open for debate."

"So be it."

He pushed himself erect and hauled her to her feet. She walked him to the door, her arm about his waist. Still he lingered.

"When I get back, there are some things we need to settle," he said.

"Such as?"

"Such as—" He hesitated, sliding the zipper on his jacket up and down its track. "Such as, what happens tomorrow? Where do we go from here?"

"Tomorrow's Monday," she replied in a careful, neutral tone. "I assume we'll both go to work—"

"Dammit, Paulette! Don't play games with me. You know what I mean."

Unfortunately she did know, and couldn't meet his gaze. She focused on the long, blunt-tipped fingers that were absently working at the zipper, and a hundred memories assailed her.

His lean, elegant hands were capable of great gentleness, and ever greater skill. They seemed to know just where to caress her, and whether to provoke or possess, tease or explore. At the moment they were displaying his uneasiness, but when he was aroused they expressed a wildness that ignited an answering wildness in her.

Looking at his hands, remembering the myriad ways he had touched her, Paulette felt a profound tenderness well up inside her—and another emotion she chose not to define.

She caught one of his hands between both of hers and held it to her cheek. "Jack," she said lightly, "whatever we have to talk about will wait till you get back."

Will you be here? He almost gave voice to the question, wondering at her nonchalance, wishing he could be as casual.

They had discussed many things since Christmas Eve, but whenever he mentioned the future, she changed the subject. He had a tendency to think out loud. He liked to spin plans for what they might be doing in two days or two weeks or two months. But Paulette didn't believe in such indulgence. Invariably she'd said, "Life's not a dress rehearsal, Jack. Let's make the most of the present."

Her elusiveness disturbed him, but when he tried to pin her down, she became even more evasive. So, for the time being at least, jogging was probably the best thing to do.

He turned his palm so that it cupped her cheek, and she stood on tiptoe and brushed a kiss across his chin.

"Go get 'em, tiger," she said. "I'll keep the home fires burning."

Reassured by her smile, he left for his workout. He had jogged three-quarters of a mile before it dawned on him that in her carefully worded farewell, Paulette had not promised she would be at his apartment when he returned.

Chapter Eleven

She was gone when he got home, but not far.

His first clue to her whereabouts was the suitcase he stumbled over just inside the vestibule; the next was that the door to Apartment Four was ajar, which meant that one of the graduate students must be back.

He was still recovering his balance when a trill of laughter from the apartment told him which one.

Three tenants shared the unit; two men and a woman. But because of marked similarities of height and weight and the androgynous way they dressed, Jonathan had trouble telling them apart.

The men were in law school. They bickered so much that Jonathan referred to them as Heckle and Jeckle.

The woman was studying for her master's degree in music. Her name was Veronica Taliaferro. "Ronnie for short," she'd told Jonathan the day she moved in. "Like the girl in the *Archie* comic books."

If one looked beyond her jeans and sweatshirts and spiky, short-cropped hair, she resembled Archie's Veronica as much as she resembled her roommates, but behind her back, everyone called her The Siren. For obvious reasons.

Her bel canto voice spanned several octaves, and in its higher registers could smash crystal.

Jonathan's entrance did not go unnoticed. Paulette called out a greeting, and Ronnie warbled an invitation to come in and have a drink.

"Thanks, I will," he said, and while Ronnie opened another wine cooler he remarked, "I wasn't expecting you for another couple of weeks."

"That was the original plan," Ronnie allowed. "But yesterday I got word that my recital's been rescheduled for the end of January, so I decided I should get down to some serious rehearsing."

"Is this your degree recital?" Paulette asked.

"Uh-huh." Ronnie underscored her agreement with a mournful roll of her brilliant dark eyes. "Once classes resume and my roommates get back, it's going to be difficult finding a place to practice."

Paulette nodded sympathetically. "That's one advantage of living alone. You can do what you like, when you like."

"As long as you can do it solo," said Jonathan. His response was automatic, as fraught with hidden meaning as Paulette's, and it made Ronnie whoop with laughter.

"You've got a point, Jon," she said, and with a broad wink at Paulette added, "I don't know about you, but the only thing I prefer to do solo is sing."

Paulette frowned as if she were startled to find herself outvoted, but before she could reply the ringing of a telephone drifted down the stairs.

"That's mine," she said. "I'd better get it."

"Hurry back," said Jonathan.

"Soon as I can."

After a smile at Ronnie, Paulette left to take the call. Fifteen minutes later, when Jonathan excused himself and crossed the hall to his own apartment, she hadn't returned.

Did she intend to?

The living room smelled of the perfume he'd given her for Christmas. Her slippers were under his bed. Her nightgown and robe were still on the hook on the bathroom door, and her toothbrush was next to his on the rack. The *TV Guide* lay facedown on the coffee table, open to the Sunday listings.

He wondered if she had watched any of the Cagney movie. Had it been an excuse?

Only embers remained of the fire in the hearth, and as he made a pyramid of birch logs and rekindled the blaze, he confronted the possibility that Paulette might make a habit of breaking her word.

They had spent three days together, and three incredible nights. In some respects he knew her as well as he knew himself. But in other ways, he had to admit he hardly knew her at all.

Jonathan tightened his hold on the poker and gave the logs a fierce prod. One of them hissed and popped, and he slouched against the mantel, staring blindly at the shower of sparks that shot up the chimney as he recalled the first time they'd made love.

He recalled his eagerness and Paulette's intriguing shyness, and remembered thinking that she was either one hell of an actress or less experienced than she pretended.

As the weekend passed, he had seen other hints that supported the hypothesis that Paulette was a swinger in name only. With a little encouragement she had become bolder, less inhibited in the bedroom, but in retrospect it seemed to him that she was holding something back.

Not with her response to his lovemaking. She was generous with her affection; loving and warm and delectably earthy. There had been moments when he was sure she cared for him. But when the physical intimacy ended, he sensed her withdrawal.

It was as if she were protecting some secret part of herself, creating barriers he dared not breach.

Perhaps it was only caution; a reluctance to make a commitment. A few reservations were natural. He had one or two himself. Or it could be that Paulette was involved with someone else.

Jonathan's lips thinned to a grim line. Much as he disliked facing this possibility, he wasn't foolish enough to think he was the first man in her life, nor was he arrogant enough to assume he would be the last.

He sighed and rubbed one hand across his eyes as he concluded that everything was speculation except for one undeniable fact: Where Paulette was concerned, it would be a mistake to assume *anything*.

JONATHAN WAS IN THE SHOWER when Paulette arrived. As she let herself into his apartment he shouted, "Be with you in a minute."

"That's all right. There's no rush." Coward that she was, she was in no hurry to say the things she had to say.

"Better yet, Paulette, why don't you join me?"

She wished she could. Heaven knew how much. But this was one time she had to resist temptation.

"Not tonight," she answered.

She sat on the edge of the sofa, hands linked about her knees, and for the hundredth time she asked herself, *How do you tell a man who's been your lover that you want to go back to being friends? How do you make him believe it, when you're not certain it's true?*

How do you avoid wounded feelings, bruised egos, recriminations?

How do you convince him you've no future together, but that the failure's not his, there's something lacking in you?

How do you confess you're not a forever kind of person without sounding melodramatic?

How do you tell him "Thanks for the memories" *without resorting to clichés?*

And why should the prospect of life without Jonathan throw her into a panic? She'd never felt that way about a man before; never even come close.

But then she'd never known a man like Jack Day before.

He turned off the shower, and a few seconds later stepped out of the bathroom. Her breath caught in her throat as she watched him stride along the hall, barechested, one towel only just preserving modesty about his hips, another at his neck.

His hair was plastered to his head in damp, unruly whorls, and when he stopped to wipe a trickle of water away from his eyes she sat up straight, steeling herself against the urge to run to him, throw her arms around him and never let him go.

Dear God! Why did doing the correct thing have to hurt so much?

"That was Anne on the phone," she said. If she stalled long enough, she might think of a way to soften her farewell.

Jonathan paused in the act of toweling his hair. "I thought maybe it was Richard."

"Richard?"

"I-miss-you-my-darling, give-me-another-chance-Richard." Jonathan flipped the towel across the back of a chair. Their gazes met and clashed. "Don't tell me you've forgotten good old Richard?"

"N-no, I haven't forgotten him, but the phone call was from Anne."

Jonathan looked as if he didn't quite believe her. *Have your fun,* his look seemed to say. *I'll go along with the gag.* "Did the newlyweds have a nice Christmas?"

Troubled by his air of mockery, Paulette made a so-so gesture with one hand.

"Uh-oh," said Jonathan. "Does this mean the honeymoon's over?"

Is he talking about us? she wondered, *or Anne and Ben?* "Not at all," she said. "At least, I don't think so. It's just that they spent Christmas with her parents, and Anne's mom and dad have this rivalry going for her attention." Paulette sighed and laced her fingers together in her lap. "Isn't it funny how a married couple can get into that cycle?"

"Yes, it is," said Jonathan, thinking of his brother and Jocelyn. "It must be rough for Anne, trying to keep the peace between them."

"Anne says the only thing that makes it possible is that she doesn't see them very often."

"How does she manage that?"

"They live in Seattle," Paulette answered. "Small world, isn't it, Jack?"

"As a matter of fact, Seattle's one subject I wanted to talk to you about."

"I'm listening," she said.

He sat at the end of the coffee table, facing her, and was immediately confronted by his own knobby knees.

They made him feel awkward, rawboned, and after a brief contemplation, he pulled the discarded towel off the chair and folded it across his thighs.

"I'm supposed to leave for Seattle tomorrow." He glanced at Paulette, gauging her response, giving her the opportunity to comment on his announcement, but she only smiled and waited for him to continue.

"It's not as if I want to go. I'm looking forward to seeing my folks, of course, but I'd much rather start the New Year with you."

"You don't have to explain, Jack. Believe me, I understand."

He realized she did. And she undoubtedly knew how much he hated leaving her. He wasn't adept at hiding his feelings, and his emotional tug-of-war must be written on his face. But by nature he was cautious. While he was showering, he had decided the prudent course of action would be to make the trip as planned. If this was more than infatuation, if their feelings for one another were genuine, they would survive the separation.

"The thing is," he said, "from January 2 till April 16, my time is not my own. I log a lot of mileage traveling to conferences with clients. I mean, we're talking major stress here. Permanent jet lag, working nonstop, living from crisis to crisis, one complication after another—"

"Taxes," said Paulette, summarizing his lament.

"Taxes," he conceded glumly.

"I can imagine you going one-on-one with the IRS." She leaned forward, elbows on her knees, chin in her hands. "I can also imagine you winning. But win, lose or draw, I'll bet you relish the fight."

Usually he did, but now the annual race to beat the deadline seemed like slow torture.

"How long will you be gone?" she asked.

"To Seattle?"

She nodded.

"Till Monday, January 4."

"A week," she murmured plaintively. It sounded like a year.

He put his arms around her and scooped her onto his lap. His own voice was ragged as he said, "Even then I'll just be in Madison to answer my mail and pick up my laundry. I'm due in L.A. January 7."

"How much time do we have?" asked Paulette.

"Till five-fifteen tomorrow. That's when my plane leaves."

"So soon?" She swayed to one side so that she could see his face. "Why didn't you mention this before?"

"I tried to, Paulette, but you wouldn't listen."

"I know, Jack, I know. I didn't want to look beyond the weekend."

"I've already canceled this trip once. I can't postpone it any longer." Her lips trembled, and he drew in a deep, steadying breath and hauled her close again. "I have to go to Seattle, babe. It's the responsible thing to do."

Responsible was not her favorite word. It brought to mind memories of a father with time to spare for his parishioners and almost none for his daughter; of a mother whose standards could never be met.

Paulette tensed momentarily, but when Jonathan kissed her she clung to him. Her body grew soft and pliant, shaping itself to his, and still cradling her in his arms, he got to his feet and started toward the bedroom.

"I'll drive you to the airport," she said.

"I'd rather we said our goodbyes here." He smiled down at her as he turned off the living-room lights, and she felt as if she might dissolve in his tenderness.

She kissed the smooth, warm skin at the base of his throat and ran questing fingertips along his collarbone, distracting him with her touch.

"Let's compromise," she said in a breathless whisper. "We'll say goodybe tonight, and tomorrow I'll drive you to the airport."

THAT NIGHT WAS LIKE A GIFT, to be cherished all the more because it was unexpected. And because it might be their last night together, she responded to Jonathan's lovemaking with a fervor that approached desperation.

With his arms around her, with the proud, hard length of his body sheltering hers, she became a creature of instinct and sensation, a stranger to herself.

She heard the hoarse endearments he uttered, heard him crooning encouragement, urging her to explore delights she'd never dreamed of, and his voice sang through her like music.

They moved in perfect synchrony, in wild harmony, to a cadence uniquely their own, and as wave after wave of pleasure coursed through her, she lost track of time and space and distance. She lost all sense of the barriers between them, and she gloried in the loss.

Was that her heart racing, or his? Was she trembling, or was he? Was his mouth caressing her, or his hands?

She had lost the ability to define where her body ended and his began, but it didn't matter. They were one flesh; one spirit possessed by the same primitive need. Nothing mattered—as long as he didn't stop.

Not now.

Not yet.

Not ever....

The next morning she was determinedly cheerful. Even when Jonathan drove her to work, her smile never wavered.

Just before they reached Shorewood, he gave her his phone number in Seattle. "In case anything comes up."

She thanked him, but made no move to write down the number.

"Don't you think you should make a note of it?" he asked.

"There's no need, Jack. I have an excellent memory."

"Humor me," he said.

At his insistence, she dug a leather-bound address book out of her shoulder bag and jotted down the number, but when he arrived at his office, he discovered she had left the book in his car.

He couldn't resist reading it. It seemed imperative that he size up the competition, but an hour of study yielded precious little information.

Paulette's handwriting wasn't easy to decipher. *E*'s resembled *I*'s. *A*'s looked like *O*'s. *U*'s, *N*'s, *V*'s and *R*'s were interchangeable. At first glance he mistook Kevin for Kiwi, Alan for Olov. And she often used abbreviations or her personal brand of shorthand, so that reading the address book was like translating a foreign language.

He had no trouble making out the asterisks beside some of the names, but he managed to interpret only portions of the accompanying notes. Just enough to drive him crazy. Gregory, for instance, had either great stamina or a speech impediment. Or maybe he had a study grant.

Some of the names had more than one asterisk; a few had none. He thumbed through the book, trying to break the code, and the instant he spotted the name *Richard*, he knew he'd found the poinsettia freak who wanted another chance.

In the first place, as near as Jonathan could tell, he was the only Richard in the book. And his was the only name with four stars. His last name was either Lowery or Laning, and aside from the street number, his address was as illegible as Paulette's comments about him.

"Great *pics*," she had written, and "pics" was underlined. Or the word might be pies or pecs, which could mean that Richard was a photographer, a pastry chef or a bodybuilder.

In this case, when in doubt, Jonathan decided to go with the most complimentary translation, and he wound up with a composite of a man who was attractive, attentive and upwardly mobile, witty (not wimpy) and sexy (not smug).

The only encouraging aspect of Richard's profile was that it was written in pencil, but when Jonathan turned to the *D*'s and saw that Paulette had entered his name in pencil too, his spirits fell.

There was nothing to distinguish Jonathan Day from the other men in her little black book. She had reduced him to a phone number with a long-distance area code and a Seattle exchange. She had made no other notations, not even an asterisk.

And the final insult was that Jack looked like Jock.

Jonathan was incensed. He wanted to run the book through the paper shredder, turn it into confetti and flush it down the toilet. He lost count of the number of times that morning he reached for the phone to call Paulette and tell her she could forget about driving him to the airport.

Once he even dialed Shorewood's number. "I can drive myself," he muttered while he waited for the switchboard operator to put him through to the registrar's office. "I don't need any favors from her."

After several rings, instead of Paulette, the operator came back on the line.

"I'm sorry, sir. The registrar's staff must be out of the office. Would you care to call back after one o'clock, or may I take a message?"

"I'll call back," he said.

But by one o'clock it had occurred to him that his entry in Paulette's address book was remarkable for its brevity.

All the other men occupied at least five lines, his name and phone number only two. And he was the only one she'd used a nickname for. Wasn't there some distinction in that? Could it mean that she didn't need descriptive tags to jog her memories of him?

At four-fifteen, on his way out of the office, he was detained by a call from an executive with a major advertising agency who wanted to film a series of TV spots featuring one of Jonathan's clients.

"I have nothing to do with professional decisions," Jonathan said. "You should be talking to his agent."

"I've been trying to reach him for the last two weeks," said the executive. "Ever since contract negotiations broke down. But all I've gotten is the runaround. He won't return my calls."

"I'd say that's your answer."

Jonathan replied in a crisp, dismissive tone, hoping to fend off further arguments, but it took another twenty minutes to convince the executive he would not intercede on the agency's behalf.

He was late arriving at Shorewood, and although Paulette was waiting for him outside Founder's Hall, they had a scant half-hour to get to Truax Field. By the time he apologized and explained the reason for the delay, there was no time left to question her about Richard or the other men she'd dated—even if she'd given him the chance.

The rush hour traffic was at its peak, and while he concentrated on driving, she chattered about her day at work, about her boss's latest trip to Florida and the scheduling problems his absence created. She didn't inquire about the address book, and Jonathan assumed she hadn't missed it.

He thought about keeping the book, and then he thought about giving it back to her. If he returned the book, she would know he had read it. He felt it burning a hole in his pocket, and couldn't decide what to do.

His flight was loading when they got to the airport. She volunteered to park the car while he checked in. He agreed, but while he waited in line, he worried about her finding a parking space in time to see him off. He was afraid they wouldn't find each other in the crowded terminal, but she came through the main entrance just as he was leaving the ticket counter.

They ran through security hand in hand, and made a dash for the boarding gate. They won their race with the clock, but his breathing was short even before he took her in his arms.

So was Paulette's.

He felt her heart drumming against his chest, felt it quicken when he kissed her.

An announcement came over the PA, and he hugged her tightly against him. "God, I'm going to miss you," he groaned.

"You'll miss your plane," she replied, ever practical. "You should go."

But her hold on him didn't slacken. For a moment longer she remained in his embrace, and he used the opportunity to slip the address book into the side flap of her shoulder bag.

Then he released her and made himself walk away.

"See you," he said, wigwagging one hand over his shoulder.

"Happy landings," Paulette called.

She sounded cheerful, unconcerned. But when he looked back, he saw that her lashes were starred with tears.

Chapter Twelve

According to Shorewood's annual *Bulletin*, the college offered "Academic excellence in a congenial atmosphere...a liberal education tailored to individual needs.

"The student comes first at Shorewood," the *Bulletin* proclaimed, and in keeping with this slogan, each employee of the college, from president to file clerk, from dean to teaching assistant, from the chief librarian to the man who cleaned cages in the lab, was expected to take a personal interest in the students.

Paulette was no exception, which was why she stopped by the campus on her way home from the airport.

The fall semester had ended December 18. The academic calendar called for grade transcripts to be in the mail by January 5. This meant that the registrar's office had to collate and process a mountain of data within the next week.

Two thousand transcripts had to be updated, grade point averages tabulated for the semester and overall. The records had to be checked, double-checked and prepared for mailing, along with probation notices for students whose cumulative averages were less than a *C*.

And with the registrar, Carl Bemis, on yet another leave of absence, the task of supervising the mailing fell to Paulette.

She didn't mind the overtime, though, or the fact that she did the work and Bemis got the credit. Seven years ago, when she had moved to Madison, he had gone out of his way to make her feel welcome. From her first day on the job he had treated her as a respected and valued addition to his staff.

In those days her family and friends had seen her as frivolous, undisciplined, unworthy of trust. Paulette supposed they still saw her that way—not that she blamed them. But from the moment they met, Carl had seen a different side of her.

He had taught her procedures, expanded her duties, broadened her insights, sought her opinion and never once doubted that she could measure up. And for the last three years, since his wife's illness had been diagnosed as Alzheimer's disease, Carl had relied on Paulette even more.

He had used up his sick leave and vacation time, and as Mrs. Bemis's condition deteriorated, he was forced to take time off without pay. He had taken his wife to specialists at most of the major medical centers in the country. He had taken her to spas and clinics. He had spent most of his savings, searching for a miracle, but nothing had slowed the insidious course of the disease.

In another year, on his sixty-third birthday, he planned an early retirement. In the meantime he lived on hope and counted on Paulette to run the registrar's office as smoothly as he had before he'd become preoccupied with his wife's failing health.

Paulette did everything she could to fulfill Carl's expectations, and her efforts did not go unrewarded.

"You're a godsend," he often told her. "I don't know what I'd do without you."

He had given her praise and promotions and constructive criticism, but what was most important, he had given her his trust, and she could not betray that. He depended on her; in return she gave him her loyalty. She owed him nothing less.

From time to time other colleges had tried to recruit her, but when opportunity came knocking, she refused to leave Shorewood.

Carl chided her about this. "Think of your future," he said. "There's no guarantee the regents will appoint you registrar after I retire."

"Don't worry about me," was her standard reply. "I can take care of myself."

Carl Bemis's devotion to his wife had shown Paulette there was more to life than career advancement. She admired her boss tremendously, but admiration and a sense of obligation were not the only reasons she was content to work that night.

If she could focus on the records, perhaps she wouldn't think about Jonathan.

The clock in the bell tower was chiming six o'clock when she parked at the foot of Shorewood Drive. Founder's Hall was quiet. Even the custodians had gone home. She let herself in the side entrance and walked along a dimly lighted corridor, past deserted offices and dark, empty classrooms, the click of her heels echoing upon the marble floor.

Earlier in the day a crew of temporaries had arranged the grade reports sequentially, by department and student ID numbers. Now the data in the card files awaited transfer to the computer.

She switched on the terminal nearest the reception counter in the registrar's office, and with a stack of index cards close at hand, set to work. But she made little headway. Her mind refused to cooperate. She sat at the terminal and kept her eyes on the screen, but it was Jonathan's image she saw.

She saw him laughing or sober or teasing, a renegade glint in his eyes. She saw his pupils dilate with passion, his features dusky and taut. She saw him relaxed or remote, pensive or playful—and oh, so very dear.

The clock struck seven, and she was startled to realize she had been staring at the same display for the last ten minutes.

Jonathan's plane had left less than two hours ago, but it seemed as if he'd been gone much longer than that. She hadn't imagined she would miss him so much. If two hours without him were this bad, how would she make it through a week?

Take it minute by minute, she thought. *One step at a time.*

She picked up a file card, entered the data, and accessed a new record on the terminal.

Over the next hour she sought refuge in routine, and her thoughts became less scattered. Insulated by silence and repetition, she went through card after card, record after record. It was tedious, but gradually the familiar amber glow of the screen induced a kind of hypnosis that dulled the pain of separation.

She had worked her way through the first batch of index cards and was finishing a second when Anne walked into the office. From her tight-lipped expression and the way she slapped her gloves onto the counter, Paulette knew she was angry even before she cried,

"I might've known I'd find you here! Have you any idea what time it is?"

Paulette sneaked a glance at her wristwatch and sprang to her feet. "It's ten-fifteen."

"Exactly." Anne snatched off her knitted toque, threw it down beside her gloves and confronted Paulette irately, tapping one snow-booted toe against the carpet. "Unless I'm mistaken, when I spoke to you yesterday you gave me your solemn word you'd phone the minute you'd talked to Jonathan."

"You're not mistaken, Anne. I'm sorry—"

"Sorry won't get you off the hook, Paulette. For the last twenty-four hours I've been beside myself with worry. I tried I don't know how many times to reach you at home. I called your friends. I looked everywhere under the sun for you. I was about to call your parents when it occurred to Ben you might be working late. So 'sorry' just won't do it; what I want is an explanation."

"I don't have one," said Paulette with a weary shake of her head. "Believe me, I wish I did."

Anne maintained her scowl a moment longer, and then her expression softened.

"How about an excuse?"

"I don't have an excuse either. All I can say is, I forgot."

"Didn't you have your talk with Jonathan?"

"We talked, Annie. It's just that our conversation didn't go the way I intended."

"But last night I got the impression you were all set to tell him you wanted to back off before either of you got serious."

"That pretty much sums up my feelings, but before I could bring the subject up, Jack announced he was leaving for Seattle."

"He's leaving? When?"

"He left today. I dropped him at the airport this afternoon."

"So you didn't break up with him?"

Paulette turned away and began rearranging the index cards, filing them in their drawer. "What would be the point? Jack will be gone till next Monday. A lot could happen between now and then. And for the next few months, he'll be on the road more often than not. Chances are he'll meet somebody else and the problem will take care of itself."

"Of course," Anne murmured. "That makes sense."

Except that Paulette looked perfectly miserable. And from what she had said about Jack Day, he was not the fickle type.

Another inconsistency was how *little* Paulette had revealed about Jack. She had always tended toward candor about the men she dated, but where Jack was concerned, she seemed inclined to keep her own counsel. Anne was aware of the fiasco at Kon-Tiki, but aside from that, although she had given Paulette plenty of openings, she'd discovered only the sketchiest details.

She could fill in some of the blanks, however. She was too much in love herself not to recognize the symptoms, and from the signs Paulette was exhibiting, she had fallen hard.

"Why don't we get out of here?" Anne suggested. "Maybe go someplace where we can discuss this."

Paulette made a choking sound and slumped against the file cabinet. Her fingers clenched about the handful of cards she was holding in a grip so fierce that her knuckles blanched.

"It's over, Annie. There's nothing to discuss. Not about Jack and me."

"But you obviously care about him."

"You're right. I do care. And that's why it has to be over."

Anne shook her head. "Don't be so hasty, Paulette. Life's full of trade-offs. There must be some alternative—"

"Not where Jack's concerned. He's looking for love. Permanence. Commitment. He'd never be satisfied with a casual affair. At least, not for long."

"Did he tell you this?"

"Not in so many words, but I know it's true." Paulette shrugged, and in a flat, despairing tone, declared, "If you met him, you'd know it, too."

"Isn't that all the more reason to hang on to him?"

"No, Annie. Don't you see? That's precisely why I have to let him go. He's looking for a wife, and I'm not ready for an exclusive contract. I don't know if I ever will be."

Anne rested her forearms on the counter and leaned forward, her face intent and thoughtful. "Paulette, you're a good judge of character and my closest friend, but you're not infallible. When it comes to judging yourself, you have this king-size blind spot."

"That's not unusual. What of it?"

"Well, if you'll think back to when Ben and I were dating, you'll recall that we had our share of misunderstandings. But you were always there for me. You listened to my troubles and gave me a shoulder to cry on, but there were times when you gave me something more practical than tea and sympathy. Do you remember one

Saturday when I called you, and I was upset because Ben hadn't phoned?"

Paulette managed a brittle smile. "Do swans float?"

"Great! And do you remember the advice you gave me? 'Give it time,' you said. 'It'll all work out in the end.' You warned me not to borrow trouble, and that's what I'm telling you."

Paulette closed the file drawer and straightened. "Okay, Anne. You've made your pitch, and I'll grant you, there are certain parallels between Ben and you and Jack and me, but there's also a major difference. You and Ben were meant for each other. You're the ideal match. You'd have made it without me playing Cupid."

"Would we? I'm not so sure."

"Well, I am. Don't underestimate yourself, Mrs. Gallagher."

"I won't if you won't."

Paulette stared at her friend, her eyes reflecting bewilderment. "You're saying I'm wrong to give up on Jack."

Anne nodded.

"And am I wrong about not wanting to lead him on?"

Anne sighed and stepped away from the counter. "I don't know, Paulette. I don't have all the answers. But I know you're terribly attracted to him, and I'm afraid, if you walk away now, you'll regret it."

"And I'm afraid I'll regret it if I don't." A spasm of anguish swept through Paulette. Her voice quavered as she said, "Jack's a decent guy, Annie. I don't want to hurt him."

"If you feel that way, what makes you think you will?"

"I *told* you, I'm not ready for marriage."

"I heard you the first time, and I think you're protesting too much," Anne replied. "Oh, I believe you don't want to hurt Jack, but the person you're really protecting is yourself. All the rest is pure hokum; what Ben would call bulltoot!"

Paulette winced at Anne's derision. Bright spots of color flamed beneath the curve of her cheekbones, and Anne skirted the counter and hurried toward her, preparing to offer an olive branch.

"Forgive me," she pleaded. "I shouldn't have been so blunt."

"It doesn't matter," said Paulette. "No hard feelings."

She felt hollow, spent. How could she sustain her anger when her thoughts and all her emotions seemed to have centered on Jonathan?

She thought of him while she reassured Anne, and again when they finally said good-night.

She thought of him while she locked the office and made her way home in his car.

She thought of him while she got ready for bed, and when she turned off the lamp and closed her eyes she saw his face; saw it so vividly, he might have been lying beside her.

She fell asleep and dreamed about him, and when she awoke the next morning, her first thought was of him. She wondered where he was, what he was doing—then, recalling the time difference, decided he must be sleeping. And she wondered if he was dreaming of her.

She thought about Jonathan at work that morning, and at noontime, when she used her lunch hour to rush back to the studio and take delivery of the furniture she had rented. And when the Colortyme van arrived, she hung over the banister and watched the movers jockey the heavy brass daybed up the stairs, fretting that they might scratch the balustrade or scuff the walls, much as Jonathan might have done if he had been there.

The men brought in the bureau, the dinette set, the desk, and while she supervised the arrangement of the pieces, she remained oddly detached, as if she were viewing the room through Jonathan's eyes.

Would he prefer the table by the windows, where it would catch the morning sun, or would he put it closer to the kitchen for efficiency's sake?

And how about the lamps?

Did he like to read in bed?

Come to think of it, did he ever read for pleasure? Was he one of those people who considered fiction a waste of time?

The movers left and she returned to Shorewood to answer the phones, read the mail and dictate a few letters. At three o'clock she took a coffee break with the staff, and afterward she spent an hour at the computer, going through the motions.

She set a goal for herself: Grace under pressure. Her heart wasn't in it, but because she had developed certain skills as a coordinator, the office ran smoothly.

On the exterior she was Roz Russell in *His Girl Friday*, all cool elegance and snappy patter. But secretly she identified with Betty Hutton in *The Perils of Pauline*. She felt as if she were flirting with disaster, clinging by her fingernails to the edge of a cliff, groping in the dark toward the light at the end of a tunnel—which inevitably would turn out to be a train.

That evening she had dinner with Anne and Ben, and when she left the Gallaghers, instead of going home, she put in another shift at the office. She stayed at Shorewood till midnight, and by the time she got home she was numb with fatigue. She fell asleep the moment her head touched the pillow, and dreamed of Jonathan again.

The next day was almost a repeat of Tuesday, except that it was interrupted by a meeting of the scholarship committee. She had lunch with her insurance agent and supper at her desk, and when she got home that night, she encountered Ronnie in the hall.

"You look beat," Ronnie observed. "Rough day?"

"Rough week," Paulette answered. And bound to get rougher unless she decided what direction to take with Jonathan.

"I was just taking a study break." Ronnie held up a cup filled with aromatic liquid. "Want to come in and have some mulled cider?"

The question caught Paulette in midyawn. "I'm a little punch-drunk so I guess I'd better pass, but thanks anyway." Halfway up the staircase, she turned to smile at her neighbor. "Could I have a rain check?"

"Anytime. You know where to find me." Paulette was fumbling through her coat pockets for her key when Ronnie added, "By the way, your phone's been ringing all evening."

Suddenly wide-awake, Paulette found the key and inserted it in the lock. "Has it?" she prompted.

"Every twenty or thirty minutes," Ronnie replied. "Last night, too."

Jack, thought Paulette. It had to be him.

Ever since he'd left on Monday, she had been waiting for his call, longing for the sound of his voice—and dreading it.

What could she say to him? What was she to do?

If only Jonathan were less responsible; or if she were more so.... But people changed, didn't they? Given the proper incentive, Jonathan might change. Or she might. It was not beyond the realm of possibility. And if there was the least chance their affair could end happily...

But that was wishful thinking, a luxury she couldn't afford.

She went into the studio, but didn't bother with the lamps. She undressed by the watery glow of the streetlight that shone through the windows, then climbed into bed and lay there, trying to sort out her feelings.

Was Anne right? Was a retreat to friendship her way of protecting herself?

She didn't have to be a mind reader to know that she was something of a novelty to Jonathan. For the time being he was fascinated. But novelty could be wearing. Fads tended to pall.

Was she afraid he would stray into the no-man's-land between love and fascination, or that he wouldn't? What if she were only a phase he was going through?

A gust of wind rattled the windows. Sleet hissed against the panes, and shivering, Paulette burrowed beneath the comforter.

Tomorrow was New Year's Eve, a time for repentance and resolution. A time for reflecting on past mistakes and planning for the future.

She'd never been good at planning ahead. She'd always relied on her instincts. But where Jonathan was concerned, she had no resolve, and her instincts seemed to falter.

Four more days, she thought. Somehow she would survive them.

But how could she bear living in the same building as Jonathan, knowing he was just downstairs, and that she must keep her distance?

New Year's Eve, she thought. And all she had to show for the old year was regrets.

THE TEMPERATURE PLUMMETED during the night. The sleet turned to snow, and by morning the streets were icy and treacherous.

Under these conditions, Paulette chose not to drive Jonathan's car.

The Metro buses were running late, and there were no taxis to be had. She wound up walking to Shorewood, bundled to the eyes against the storm. It was nine-thirty before she made it to the office, almost ten o'clock before she had thawed out enough to begin work.

One of the temporaries gave her a handful of memos, among them a message that Jonathan Day had phoned from Seattle.

For a few minutes Paulette sat at her desk, paralyzed by indecision, then she slipped Jonathan's message beneath the corner of the blotter. At intervals throughout the morning, she picked up the message and read it as if she might have overlooked something in her other readings. But when the rest of the staff left at noon, she still had not returned Jonathan's phone call.

IT WAS RAINING IN SEATTLE, a cold, relentless drizzle that threatened to continue all weekend.

New Year's Eve, thought Jonathan. But he was in no mood to celebrate.

He stood at the patio door in his parents' kitchen, contemplating gray skies, gaunt trees and waterlogged shrubs, wondering what Paulette would be doing tonight and who she'd do it with.

Would she give Richard another chance for the sake of auld lang syne? Would she watch the New Year in with one of the jocks he'd seen at her housewarming?

He imagined her dancing to Guy Lombardo in the arms of another man. He imagined her partner folding her close, kissing her....

Dammit! Why didn't she call?

The doorbell rang, but Jonathan remained at the window. The bell rang again, and then twice more, his brother's imperious summons. Jonathan heard his father's footsteps cross the foyer, the rumble of voices in the hall, and a moment later the swinging door from the dining room opened and his mother came into the kitchen.

"Larry and Jocelyn are here," she announced. "We're about ready to leave."

"Give Aunt Trudy my best," said Jonathan. He didn't turn around.

"She'll be disappointed, dear. You've always been her favorite."

"The feeling's mutual," he said.

"If you'd like to come with us, we'll wait for you to change."

Jonathan shoved his hands deeper into his pants pockets and considered his mother's suggestion. He usually enjoyed his family's get-togethers, but the thought of spending this particular evening with his relatives made him feel claustrophobic.

"No, don't wait," he replied. "If I decide to join the party, I'll catch up with you later, at the club."

"Very well, dear. If you're sure—"

"I'm positive, Mom."

Charlotte Day studied her son, a tiny furrow between her brows. Jonathan was not behaving at all like himself, and she was at a loss to explain the change. Something was troubling him, that much was clear. But what could it be?

A few hours earlier she'd caught him prowling near the telephone again, and she had inquired about the obvious possibilities. She could only assume Jonathan had responded honestly.

No, he'd told her, he didn't mind the weather. The rain made him feel at home. And business was fine. "Better than fine, it's booming," he said. "This has been the best year ever. I have all the clients I can handle and a waiting list besides."

So the rain hadn't dampened his spirits, and he wasn't concerned about money. And now, in answer to her question, he denied that he was worried about Larry and Jocelyn.

"Haven't you noticed them trading insults?" she asked.

Jonathan admitted he had. "It's hard to miss," he allowed. "Yesterday at Hurricane Ridge they did more fighting than skiing."

"Larry ought to spend more time with Jocelyn," said Charlotte. "He takes her for granted, and she lets him. Instead of telling him what's bothering her, she takes potshots and feels sorry for herself."

"I'm sure it's only temporary," said Jonathan. "They'll work it out."

"Will they? I wonder—Sometimes I think they're too much alike."

A hint of annoyance had crept into Charlotte's voice, but Jonathan didn't hear it. He was frowning at the reflection of the wall phone in the window glass, willing the phone to ring.

For all his questions concerning Paulette's whereabouts, he was certain of only one fact. She was never at home to take his calls.

Who was she spending her time with? One of the men in her date book? Someone new? Did she ever think about last weekend? Did she ever think of him, or had she forgotten—?

"It's a woman, isn't it?"

Jonathan glanced at his mother, startled.

"Is she married?"

"Good Lord, Mother! What makes you ask that?"

"You've been so distracted. I just thought—"

"She's not married," Jonathan cut in. "You can put your mind at ease on that score. I'm through carrying the torch for Jocelyn."

"I'm relieved to hear it, son."

"Not half as relieved as I am to say it. But sometimes I feel as if I've jumped from the frying pan into the fire."

"I see," said Charlotte. "And this woman you've met is responsible?"

Jonathan rested his forehead against the patio door and closed his eyes. "Her name's Paulette. Paulette D'Amboise. She's a tenant in my building, and she's the most baffling, frustrating, out-and-out irritating woman I've ever known."

Sounds promising, Charlotte thought. And since Jonathan wasn't watching, there was no need to hide her delight. She smiled and tucked a stray curl into place.

"Paulette," she murmured. "What a lovely name! Tell me more about her."

Chapter Thirteen

The unthinkable happened on the way to the airport, while Paulette was cruising along East Johnson Street, minding her own business.

All afternoon, inside her head, an imaginary clock had been ticking off the minutes till Jonathan's plane got in, and now, less than twenty minutes from touchdown, she was a bundle of conflicting emotions, excited by the thought of seeing him again, yet dreading their reunion.

She had done a lot of soul-searching over the New Year weekend, but still wasn't certain how to handle her predicament. Admittedly she was a bit preoccupied, but she wasn't speeding. She wasn't dawdling, either. She was driving with the traffic, aware of the slippery conditions, keeping a safe distance from the car ahead, when a station wagon came skidding through the stop sign at the intersection with North Baldwin.

Paulette pumped the brakes and veered toward the curb, swerving to the rear of the station wagon. The tires screeched; she felt the wheels lock and lose traction as the sports car lurched onto the ice. Then she was spinning, and in the milliseconds before the collision she thought *This can't be happening. It's a nightmare.*

But it was real.

She heard horns blaring, glass splintering, a grinding crash of metal that seemed to go on forever, and then she absorbed the impact, felt it jar her spine. The shoulder harness dug into her chest, abrading the side of her neck as her head pitched forward, then back. Her teeth clicked together and cut into her tongue. Her ears rang, and when the ringing subsided there was silence and a circle of faces peering in at her and the awful rending shriek of the door opening as hands reached in to unbuckle her seat belt and voices calling, "Is she all right?"

"I'm okay," she said. "Just shaken up."

Someone helped her out of the car, and the driver of the station wagon pushed through the crowd.

"Allow me," he said. His face was ashen and shiny with sweat, and the arm he offered was none too steady as he guided her toward the curb.

One of the witnesses found a flashlight and began directing traffic. Another notified the police. A third surveyed Paulette and the other driver and suggested calling an ambulance.

"Not for me," said the station wagon man.

"Me either," said Paulette. She felt bruised, numb and slightly queasy from the taste of blood, but her injuries were minor.

She huddled with the other driver on the curb, shivering in the cold while they waited for the police to arrive. Some good Samaritan brought them blankets, and after a while the station wagon man began reliving the accident, ranting about glare ice and trying to steer out of the skid, threatening to sue the city for not sanding the street.

Paulette listened to his raving, but none of it sank in. She was distracted by thoughts of Jonathan, remembering how much he loved his car, the pride with which he had shown it to her, the way he'd boasted about keeping the engine in racing tune.

A patrol car appeared, along with a tow truck. The station wagon man interrupted his tirade and went off to speak to the officers, but Paulette stayed at her post on the curb.

Jonathan would be at the airport by now, expecting her to pick him up. She thought about finding a phone, leaving a message that she had been detained, but that seemed too easy. Too impersonal. Her conscience would not let her do it.

She watched the policemen pacing off distances, the station wagon man yapping at their heels, and all she could think was that this incident was worse than the time she'd thought Jonathan was proposing; worse than dumping coffee in his shoe.

Never mind that the accident wasn't her fault. He would be furious when he discovered she had demolished his car. He'd never forgive her. He'd probably be sorry they'd ever met. But the least she could do was tell him about the accident face-to-face, so that he could read her the riot act.

The tow truck driver, a burly moon-faced man in greasy overalls, was assessing the damage to the sports car. One of the policemen joined him, and after a good deal of gesturing and head scratching, the officer retrieved Paulette's handbag from the passenger seat and turned his attention to her.

"Evening, Miss—"

"D'Amboise." She spelled her last name, slurring over the letters, and after handing her the purse, the officer made a notation on his clipboard.

"Driver's license, please."

She found her billfold and removed the license without prompting. "How bad—?" Her lips, her tongue felt swollen, so thick she could hardly talk.

The officer eyed her above his clipboard. "Have you been drinking, miss?"

She denied this with an emphatic shake of her head, and grimaced as pain lanced through her neck. Moving more cautiously, she pantomimed writing, and the officer gave her his pen and attached a fresh sheet of paper to his clipboard.

With the policeman looking over her shoulder, she wrote, "Bit my tongue."

He squinted at the sentence, puzzled by her hasty scrawl. "Bet my fanny? Is that a yes?"

"No," she wrote, and in clear block letters, reprinted the message. He nodded his understanding, and she printed, "How bad is the car?"

"It'll have to be towed," he said.

"That's a fact," said the driver of the tow truck, ambling up beside them. "You can see for yourself the front quarter panel's dragging against the wheel." Waving a grimy hand toward the wreckage, he added, "It's a doggone shame, ma'am. She must've been a beauty. But a little body work'll fix 'er up, right as rain."

Paulette stared at the sports car, gripped by a misery too deep for tears, and the truck driver fished a crumpled dispatch form from a pocket in his coveralls.

"Now, ma'am, where'd you like me to take 'er?"

"Dunno. Where's good?"

The truck driver scratched his head at Paulette's barely articulate reply, and the policeman spoke up.

"How about Smitty's? I've heard they're good."

"Yup," said the driver, "and they specialize in those foreign jobs, but they're not cheap."

Both men glanced at Paulette, leaving the decision to her. She pulled the clipboard closer and printed, "Want the best."

"Okay," said the driver. "Smitty's it is." He wrote *Smitty's Garage* on his form and copied Paulette's name and address from the accident report. "All I need now is your insurance."

Paulette entered her agent's name and the policy number in the appropriate blanks, and the driver stuffed the form into his pocket.

"That about wraps 'er up," he declared.

"Jus' one thing," Paulette confessed in a cracked whisper. "Car's not mine."

The driver gave her a befuddled look. The policeman demanded, "Whose is it?"

"It's mine, officer."

The answer was issued in a thundering baritone that seemed to vibrate with rage. From the corner of her eye, Paulette caught a glimpse of a taxi drawn up at the curb, and the tall, dark-haired man striding toward them—

Jonathan!

She whirled around for a better look at him, and pain shot through the back of her neck, sharp and dizzying. She swayed on her feet. Her head was reeling. There was a rushing sound in her ears. White-hot sparks erupted in front of her eyes, then the world tilted on its axis and everything went dark.

She felt herself sliding, falling, and in the moment before she blacked out, somebody shouted, "Catch her! She's going to faint."

A hand clutched at her wrist. Strong arms supported her at the waist and knees. Somehow she knew they were Jonathan's. After that, for a time she knew nothing until she came to in the back seat of the patrol car, with her head on Jonathan's shoulder.

She tried to sit up, but he defeated her struggles with a gentle, all-encompassing grasp.

"Try not to move," he said. "We're taking you to the hospital."

"No need," she mumbled. The heavy wool of his topcoat muffled her objection, but she hadn't the energy to lodge another protest.

Jonathan was stroking her hair. She felt the hard warmth of his palm against her cheek, and a strange lassitude stole through her. Close to him she felt safe. So safe. The least movement seemed to require too much effort, so she closed her eyes and let the darkness enfold her.

The lights in the emergency room revived her. While Jonathan dealt with the paperwork, she was strapped to a transport cart, and with one arm bound to an IV, the other by a blood pressure cuff, she was whisked to an examining cubicle.

"CBC and chem panel, stat," said the doctor. He waved his hand in front of Paulette's face. "How many fingers?"

She held up two fingers on her right hand.

"Good," said the doctor. "Let's see you squeeze them."

"Pleasure," she mumbled, and grabbing his fingers, she squeezed as hard as she could.

"Excellent. Now the other hand." The doctor peered into her eyes, her ears, her mouth. "Oh-oh. What have we here?"

"Ay 'ongue," she mumbled.

The doctor smiled and called for x-rays, and while they waited for the technicians to adjust the equipment, he tested her reflexes and began jabbing a pin into her feet.

At first Paulette merely withdrew, but when the pinpricks moved to her ankles, she expressed herself more strenuously. "Why're you poking around down there? It's my neck that hurts."

The complaint was garbled, but the doctor understood it. He explained that the combination of neck pain and loss of consciousness required a thorough neurological exam. "We need to rule out head and vertebral injuries," he said.

He finished his evaluation, then left to check on the lab tests and x-rays, and Jonathan and the younger of the police officers came into the cubicle.

"I have to get your statement," the policeman told Paulette. "Do you feel up to answering a few questions?"

She responded with a dispirited stare. How could she answer questions when her tongue refused to function?

"Can't this wait?" Jonathan asked.

"It could, but I think we already have most of the details straight." Turning to Paulette, the officer suggested she blink her eyes. "Once for yes, twice for no."

She shut her eyes, then opened them, indicating her willingness, and the interrogation began. She lay there blinking and blinking, agreeing with some things, refuting others, clinging to Jonathan's hand all the while.

He looked rumpled and tired, as haggard as she felt—as if he hadn't slept for a week. If she could talk she would tell him how sorry she was. She would ask about his car.

"Don't worry about the Cobra," he said as if he'd read her mind. "What's important is that you're not seriously hurt."

The laboratory studies confirmed this; so did the x-rays. And the blood alcohol was negative, which concluded the police investigation. Both officers wished her a speedy recovery and left the emergency room.

"Your tests are normal, except for an elevated white blood cell count," said the doctor. "With trauma, that's not unusual. We'd like you to keep track of your temperature for the next day or two, to be on the safe side, but the white count probably means that your body's gearing up in case you have to fight off an infection."

He went on to say that her abrasions and contusions were superficial. They should heal quickly. The neck sprain would take a bit longer. "Is there someone who can take care of you?" he asked.

"There's me," Jonathan replied.

"She'll need hourly neuro checks tonight," said the doctor. "And we're talking about at least a week of bed rest. Maybe two."

"I'll be in town till Wednesday," Jonathan replied. "After that, I'll make other arrangements."

"Would that be all right with you, Paulette?"

She blinked and tightened her grip on Jonathan's hand, and the doctor nodded, satisfied.

He gave her a cervical collar, samples of muscle relaxants and analgesics, prescribed ice for her tongue, heat and massage to relieve the spasms in her neck, and released her to Jonathan's care.

The taxi ride home was torture. Whenever the cab hit a pothole, pain stabbed through Paulette's neck. But by the time they arrived at the apartment building, the medication she'd been given in the emergency room was beginning to take effect.

Her knees wobbled as Jonathan helped her along the front walk. Without him, she'd never have made it up the porch stairs.

"I'm taking you to my place," he declared.

She blinked owlish agreement, too woozy to care where she spent the night.

Her legs gave way at the door to his apartment. He caught her before she sank to the floor and carried her inside, through the living room and along the hall to the bedroom. He deposited her on the bed gently, mindful of her injuries, removed her boots and stockings and helped her out of her coat.

"Can you manage the rest of your clothes, Paulette?"

She blinked once for yes, and he said he was going to get a few of her things from the studio. "Anything special you'd like?" he asked.

She tried to tell him she was thirsty, but couldn't pronounce the words. She pantomimed holding a water glass, but when she pretended to be drinking from it, the attempt to raise her hand to her mouth triggered a spasm so severe that she listed to one side. Only Jonathan's support kept her from toppling against the headboard.

"Easy, Paulette. Take it easy."

He propped pillows around her, and when she was steady, he told her he'd bring her a pencil and notepad and left the room.

Once alone, Paulette discovered other limitations.

Getting out of her skirt was simple enough. She merely unfastened the button and zipper, then stood up and allowed the skirt to fall to a puddle about her ankles. She even contrived to pick up the skirt and hang it over the bedpost. But any movement that required stretching or twisting was beyond her.

She sat at one end of the bed, overcome by a sense of helplessness. She couldn't talk, could barely make a fist, and she couldn't pull her sweater over her head.

If she had been more alert she might've felt chagrined, but Jonathan made self-consciousness unnecessary.

He brought her robe and helped her into it, then turned back the covers and tucked her into bed. He brought her a glass of warm milk. He brought her some chipped ice for her tongue, and through all this he was gruff and matter-of-fact, as if he were accustomed to tending ladies in distress.

Everything went smoothly until he offered to spend the night in the living room. "You'll rest more comfortably if you have the bed to yourself," he said.

Paulette blinked twice for no and reached for the notepad. "I'll sleep better if you're here," she printed.

"Do you mean it?" he asked.

"What do you want?" she printed. "A testimonial?"

Jonathan laughed. "I'd be out of luck if I did. You're in no condition to give me one."

Paulette fought back a yawn. She thought she'd heard uncertainty in Jonathan's laughter, but she was too groggy to follow up on it. For now all she wanted was sleep.

JONATHAN SAT WITH PAULETTE till she dozed off. Even after she had fallen asleep, he stayed in the bedroom.

Her doctor had told him to wake her every hour and make sure she was responding normally. He'd also said the medicines he'd prescribed would induce six to eight hours of light sedation, but Jonathan wanted to be sure she was comfortable.

Besides, he enjoyed looking at her when she was unaware of his scrutiny. The curve of her lips, her long silky lashes, the bright spill of curls that nestled against her cheek gave him pleasure.

He'd done a good deal of thinking over the New Year weekend and in the course of his deliberations he had realized that love was not a footrace or a trophy to be won. It had to be given freely, without reservations and without coercion, which meant that it was senseless to be jealous of Paulette's past.

Once he had decided this, he stopped kidding himself that the men in her address book were the source of his anxiety. Paulette's experience, or the lack of it, wasn't important.

What made him frantic was the guessing game they'd been playing, and he had boarded the plane in Seattle determined to have it out with her, tell her how he felt about her and find out how she felt about him.

But having come this far, he could wait.

Tomorrow he would notify Paulette's parents that she'd been in an accident, and sometime before he had to leave on Wednesday afternoon, he and Paulette would have their talk.

In the meantime, it was enough to know that she was here—in his room, in his bed—and that he was falling in love with her.

THAT NIGHT SET THE PATTERN for the next thirty-six hours. Jonathan prepared Paulette's meals. He ran her bath and helped her into the whirlpool. He gave her massages, read to her, and saw that she took her medicine on time. He was attentive, caring and sweet, and the sweeter he was, the more troubled her conscience became.

By Wednesday morning the swelling in her tongue had subsided. She was curled up on the bed, having a second cup of coffee, and Jonathan was packing for his trip to Los Angeles when she decided they'd had enough communicating with notes and gestures. It was time to break the silence.

"I wish you'd yell at me and get it over with," she said.

Jonathan stared at her, taken aback by the outburst. "Why would I want to yell at you?"

"Because I wrecked your car."

He dropped his shaving kit on top of his suitcase, and in two long strides crossed to the bed. "For God's sake, Paulette! What kind of monster do you think I am?"

She set her cup and saucer on the nightstand, unable to endure the reproach she saw in his eyes. "I don't think you're a monster, but you're not a saint, either. You must be angry with me. I know how much that car means to you."

"Forget the car! I don't give a damn about it as long as you're going to be all right. Don't you know how much I—?"

"Wait, Jack! Before you say anything else, there's something I have to tell you."

His features taut and expectant, Jonathan sat beside her and took her hand, lacing his fingers through hers. "Go on," he said. "I'm listening."

"Maybe I've mentioned this before, but one reason I took a sublet was that I've been waiting for my insurance claim to be settled."

"Yes, I'm aware of that."

"Well, what you don't know is, last week I got the check."

"And?"

"And—well, I've sort of begun looking at condos."

The expectation drained from Jonathan's face. "I see," he replied without inflection. "Find anything you like?"

"As a matter of fact, there is one place that has definite possibilities. Two bedrooms, two baths, full dining room, underground garage—It's really quite charming, and it's in my price range."

"I see," he repeated in the same mechanical tone. "Am I to assume this is your way of giving notice that you won't be renewing your lease?"

"N-no, not exactly. I haven't made an offer yet, but I'm going to. It's either that or pay capital gains on the settlement. I don't have a choice."

"But you do, Paulette. There are a number of options."

"Name one."

"To begin with, you have a year before the taxes are due, so the most obvious choice would be to let the money work for you. I'd be happy to recommend some investments that should pay handsome dividends, which would give you more leverage when you do buy another condo."

Paulette's jaw dropped. Fool that she was, she had thought Jonathan's options would be romantic rather than practical. How could he look at her as if she were the embodiment of all his dreams, and talk about leverage?

"Thanks for the advice," she said, "but where would I live in the meantime?"

"You could stay here—"

Never, she thought. The addition of the rental furniture made the studio seem less barren, but she couldn't live there; not a day, not a minute longer than she had to.

She eyed Jonathan warily, and it dawned on her that, while her attention had drifted, he had continued talking.

"Beg pardon?"

"I was just saying you could stay here, Paulette. With me."

"You mean live together?"

He grinned. "That's another way of putting it."

She stirred against the pillows, feeling an awkwardness that had nothing to do with her bruises or scrapes or the padded cervical collar she was wearing.

"I don't want to scare you off," he added. "I'd like to make it clear that I'm not suggesting a permanent arrangement. I'm willing to settle for a trial period. Say two months."

"Two *months*?"

His grin acquired a rakish slant. "Just pretend it's a long weekend."

Don't do it, warned a shrill inner voice. *Don't even think about it.* But some perverse part of herself wouldn't let her say no. Instead she murmured, "I don't know what to say, Jack. I haven't lived with anyone since college."

"Neither have I, but we can't let that stop us. We have something special, Paulette. Too special to let it slip away. At least that's how I feel, and I think you feel the same way. Last week in Seattle, I couldn't get you out of my mind. I can't stop thinking about you—wanting you—loving you—"

Jonathan lifted her hand and touched his lips to the inside of her wrist. "That's why it seems like a good idea for us to try living together, but whatever happens in our relationship, if you'll consider my proposition, I'm sure you'll agree it could work to your advantage."

If only she could believe it would work at all! But a Christmastime project was one thing; living with Jonathan was quite another. Living together meant emotional intimacy. It meant sharing and compromise and sacrifice.

What if, at the end of two months, Jonathan wanted to say goodbye and she wanted more?

I've waited too long, she thought. *If I say no, I'll hurt Jack. If I say yes, I'll be the one who's hurt.*

She exhaled a sigh, and sensing her foreboding, Jonathan bent down and kissed her softly on the mouth.

"You don't have to give me your answer now," he said. "We'll keep in touch while I'm in California. But whether your answer is yes or no, I hope you won't rush into anything with the condo. Making an offer, buying your own place seems—I don't know, Paulette. It just seems so final."

Chapter Fourteen

Paulette had played enough chess to recognize a stalemate when she saw one, and *final* seemed too gentle a word for such a gambit.

But then, Jonathan was gentle. Above all else, he was a gentle man.

She watched him walk back and forth between the bureau and the closet, collecting shirts and suits and ties, packing them in his garment bag, and she knew they had reached an impasse.

Why wait? Why not tell him now that she couldn't move in with him? If she'd cared about him less she might have risked it. But she did care. And postponing her decision wouldn't change the way she felt about him. It wouldn't change her.

She trailed her fingers over her mouth as if she might recreate the warmth of Jonathan's lips, and followed his every move as he locked the garment bag and crossed to the bureau. He opened his briefcase to make a last-minute check of the documents inside, and she watched him go through his files, avidly storing up memories, envying the ease with which he compartmentalized his life—and resenting it.

Minutes ago he had told her he couldn't get her out of his mind. Then he had issued what amounted to an ultimatum. Now all he could think about was his clients.

He glanced up and caught her studying him.

"I wish you didn't have to leave, Jack."

"So do I, Paulette, but I have to make this trip." His shoulders rose in a conciliatory shrug. "It's the responsible thing to do."

What about me? she wanted to ask. But petulance wouldn't solve anything, and so she smiled and picked up her coffee cup.

Had Jonathan actually told her he loved her, or had she only imagined it?

She peered at the dregs of coffee in her cup, trying to recall word for word what he had said. When the intercom buzzed, she hardly noticed him leaving the room, and she remained lost in thought till he returned.

"There's someone here to see you," he said, and before she could assimilate his announcement, her mother stepped through the doorway.

Paulette's first reaction was to leap to her feet, but her injuries made leaping impossible. She barely managed to sit up as her mother sailed toward her, urging her to lie back and be comfortable.

Since Paulette was in no condition to argue, she complied with her mother's instructions. Jonathan, she noted, looked terribly pleased with himself.

"Are you surprised?" he asked.

"I'm—speechless." *And Mother must be horrified to find me in Jack's bed, wearing his pajama top.*

With typical brisk efficiency, Eileen D'Amboise was bustling about, adjusting the draperies against the morning glare, smoothing wrinkles out of the bedspread, and to Paulette each movement seemed a reprimand.

She folded the lapels of her robe higher about her throat and held her breath, waiting for the lecture to begin. The atmosphere in the room was so thick with constraint, she marveled that Jonathan didn't feel it. But he only said he had some phone calls to make, and with an engaging smile at her mother, left them alone.

Eileen plumped the pillows, then laid her hand against Paulette's forehead. "I do believe you have a fever. Is there a thermometer?"

"On the nightstand. But I don't have a fever, Mother. Jack took my temperature earlier."

Eileen raised her eyebrows. "You call him Jack?"

"Is there any reason I shouldn't?"

"No, dear, except that your young man did say he prefers to be called Jonathan."

Telltale splotches of color blossomed in Paulette's cheeks. "He never told me that, and he's not my young man."

Her mother's eyebrows rose a notch higher. "You're awfully flushed. Are you sure you don't have a fever?"

"I'm positive."

"Then perhaps you're embarrassed."

"And I suppose you're not?"

"No, Paulette, nor am I scandalized or even mildly amazed."

But Eileen was tenacious, and would not be satisfied until she had taken Paulette's temperature. She shook down the thermometer and thrust it at her daughter. Paulette pushed it aside.

"Let's stop fencing, Mother. Why don't you tell me what you really think?"

"Well, if you must know, I think your staying here is the most convenient arrangement while you're recuperating. But for your own sake, I hope that eventually you'll decide to marry Jonathan."

"You're jumping the gun," Paulette answered crossly. "He hasn't asked me."

"Ah, but he will." Eileen made this prediction with maddening confidence, and popped the thermometer into Paulette's mouth, effectively muzzling her. "Now I'm going to get your medicine, and after that you can have a nice nap before lunch."

Paulette didn't want to take a nap. She wanted to stay awake so that she could provide a buffer between Jonathan and her mother, but within minutes of taking the pills her eyelids started to droop.

Through the half-open door to the hallway she could hear Eileen and Jonathan in the living room, discussing family resemblances. Jonathan asked if there were other redheads among the D'Amboises, and Eileen said, "None that I'm aware of, but in personality, Paulette's the image of my mother."

"How so?"

"She was a rebel too, an eighties woman trapped by the double standards of the twenties. Her idol was Isadora Duncan, and her greatest ambition was to become a dancer."

"And did she?"

"Yes, at a cost. Her parents wouldn't hear of her going on the stage. In those days, well-bred young ladies didn't do that sort of thing. So she took a job as a bookkeeper in a dance studio to pay her tuition."

"She sounds like quite a woman."

"She was," Eileen agreed. "Or so I've been told. I never knew her very well. She never married, you see.

She was too wrapped up in her career. And when I was born, she left me with her sister—"

Eileen lapsed into silence, and when Jonathan spoke, he lowered his voice. Eileen answered quietly, so that Paulette couldn't eavesdrop, but she had heard enough to know that they didn't need a buffer.

She was almost asleep when her mother came in to check on her. "Jonathan's taking me on a tour of the building," Eileen said. "After that, we're going to the supermarket. Can I get you anything before we leave?"

"No, thanks." Paulette looked at Eileen with some bemusement. "I heard you talking to Jack," she said. "You've never told me nearly as much about your mother."

"Yes, well, I wasn't sure you'd be interested, and Jonathan's a good listener."

"You like him, don't you?"

"Very much. Do you find that incredible?"

Paulette didn't. Not really. And for the remainder of the morning she wondered why.

Over lunch she found out the approval was mutual. Jonathan and her mother chatted about renovating old houses and restoring antiques, and while they explored common interests, it occurred to Paulette that there were quite a few similarities between Jonathan and her parents.

She recalled the night she met Jack, and remembered her impression that he was the kind of man her mother and father introduced her to whenever she went home, and she felt a bit like Dorothy discovering the Wizard of Oz was just a snake-oil salesman with a trunkful of magic tricks.

Her appetite deserted her. After a few bites, she picked at the rest of her omelet. And after lunch, while

Eileen was loading the dishwasher and Jack was waiting for the airport limousine, their easy give-and-take continued.

Here was further proof, if Paulette needed it, of how incompatible she and Jonathan were. How could she hope to get along with a man who got along with her mother?

She made her way back to the bedroom without assistance, and when the limousine arrived and Jonathan came in to say goodbye, she pretended to be asleep.

He approached the bed. She felt him standing over her, watching her, and regretted the deception. But she kept her eyes shut.

Jonathan leaned down and kissed her forehead, her temple, the bridge of her nose.

"Give it up," he whispered. "I know you're faking."

He kissed her mouth, and she couldn't help responding. Her lips softened, parted, molded themselves to his, and her fingers curled into fists beneath the blankets.

She wanted to hold on to him, keep him from leaving. She wished he would ask her to go to Los Angeles with him. If he asked, she would follow wherever he went and never look back.

He straightened, and her eyes flew open.

"You'll call me?"

"Tonight," he promised. "As soon as I get to the hotel." He stroked her cheek, and with a gentle forefinger closed her eyelids. "Dream of me, Paulette."

"I will." *Always,* she thought. *Only stay with me. Don't go.*

A few hours ago, Jonathan had said he loved her. In a world where that could be true, surely anything was possible.

But when she opened her eyes, he was gone.

Chapter Fifteen

Paulette spent the rest of that afternoon and evening waiting for Jonathan's phone call. By the time it came there was no way it could live up to her expectations. Their conversation was stilted, filled with small talk about his trip, the West Coast weather, his plans for tomorrow.

Neither of them mentioned his proposal that she move in with him.

She had been desolate before the call, and felt more desolate when it was over. Long-distance, she realized, was no substitute for being with Jonathan, and for the next two days she couldn't eat, couldn't sleep, and scarcely spoke to her mother.

By Saturday evening Eileen was at her wit's end. She had tried everything she could think of—patience and impatience, understanding, scolding, cajolery, bribery. But even a batch of fluffer-nutters didn't penetrate her daughter's apathy.

Paulette rarely left the bedroom. She stopped taking her medicine. She refused the massages and passive exercise her doctor had prescribed. She lived from phone call to phone call, and drove her mother to despair.

Over the telephone Eileen discussed the situation with Paul D'Amboise, and he suggested prayer.

"I've been praying," she told him. "I pray constantly that Paulette will get better, but so far there's no sign of improvement."

"Pray for strength then, and remember, 'This too shall pass.'"

"Listen, my darling," Eileen said, "I'm speaking to you as my husband, not as my spiritual adviser. I hoped you would respond in the same way, so please, *please* stop quoting Lincoln and tell me what to do."

"I wish I could, but as you well know, Paulette has always been a mystery to me. Why don't you try that friend of hers? You know, the girl who just got married."

"Anne Gallagher? Of course! I'll phone her right away."

As soon as she'd finished the call to her husband, Eileen consulted Anne, who listened sympathetically and recommended work.

"Paulette's had too much time to think," Anne said. "She needs something to take her mind off Jonathan. If you like, I could stop by the registrar's office on Monday and pick up some of the scholarship committee files. If anything can distract her, they will."

"I suppose it's worth a try," Eileen conceded doubtfully, wondering what she should do in the meantime.

The answer came from an unexpected quarter that same evening, when Ronnie Taliaferro stopped by with a jug of homemade raspberry cordial.

"My father bottled this the year I was born," she told Eileen. "I've been saving it till I get my degree, only now it looks as if that may never happen."

"Don't be silly, my dear. I've heard you singing. You have a lovely voice."

"When I'm feeling soprano I do, but today my mood is basso profundo."

"Why? What's the problem?"

"My accompanist has the flu."

"Aren't there any other pianists who could help you out?"

"Oh, sure. Scads of 'em. But I don't know a single one who'll be in town before the spring semester starts, and that's more than a week away, which leaves me up on the proverbial scatological creek. I'm already on a tight schedule. Absolutely every day counts. But without an accompanist I can't rehearse, without rehearsals I can't perform, and without a performance I can kiss the degree goodbye. So the only thing left to do is drown my sorrows in this fine old liqueur."

"I don't believe sorrow dissolves in alcohol," Eileen cautioned.

Ronnie rolled her eyes toward the ceiling. "The voice of reason," she intoned. "Just what I needed."

"Don't we all?" said Eileen. "Now, what else can I do for you?"

"Well, all I've got is jelly jars, and Daddy's liqueur deserves better than that."

Eileen smiled and led the way to the kitchen. "Let's see what we can find in Jonathan's cupboards."

"I could also use some company, and I figured you could too. You've been cooped up here since Wednesday—"

"Say no more." Eileen removed a pair of cordial glasses from the corner cabinet and held them so that they caught the light. "Will these do?"

Ronnie made a droll face. "They'd make gorgeous thimbles, but I don't think they're suitable for drowning."

Eileen changed one of the cordial glasses for a wineglass. "I believe I'll stick to the thimble," she explained. "I don't have much tolerance for alcohol."

Ronnie's trill of laughter made the chandelier chime. "That, Mrs. D'Amboise, is the general idea."

But after one sip of the liqueur, Ronnie slid her glass along the coffee table toward Eileen. "Tastes like cough syrup," she said. "If you like it, it's all yours."

Eileen did like the cordial. It reminded her of cherry soda. And she liked Ronnie Taliaferro. She liked Ronnie's puckish sense of humor, her cheerfulness in the face of adversity, the good-natured affection with which she regarded her parents. She liked Ronnie's laughter and her rich fluting voice that sounded like bird song. But most of all, Eileen liked Ronnie because Ronnie accepted her as an equal—woman to woman, not woman to fossil.

They sat in Jonathan's living room and talked and joked and drank—Ronnie a beer, Eileen the liqueur—and by the time her wineglass was empty, Eileen felt as if she had found a long-lost friend. After the second glass, she invited Ronnie to call her Eileen, and after the third she lost track of how much she'd had to drink.

She didn't know which of them suggested turning on the stereo, but music seemed an excellent idea. It made the occasion seem more festive, almost like a party. Chicago jazz was a trifle raucous, but if the commotion they made disturbed Paulette, so what?

As Ronnie said, "If Paulette wants to mope, let her. After what she's been through, she's got a right to sing the blues. But what purpose would it serve for you to deny yourself a little fun?"

Given her fuzzy-minded state, this was precisely the advice Eileen wanted to hear, and just before midnight, when Paulette emerged from the bedroom to complain about the noise, she found her mother barefoot and giggling, giddy as a schoolgirl, cavorting about the living room.

"What in the world is going on?" she demanded.

"Your mom's teaching me to do the Charleston," Ronnie caroled. "Would you care to join us?"

"At this hour? I think not."

"She thinks not," Eileen muttered, returning her daughter's glare. The moment the words were out, she hiccuped and collapsed onto the sofa.

"Why, mother! You've been drinking!"

"You noticed. Good for you."

"But that's not like you. Dad would be shocked if he saw you this way."

"How would you know? You don't know the first thing about your dad and me."

Paulette drew in a ragged breath, startled by her mother's belligerence. "Perhaps it's time I learned," she said.

"Perhaps you'd better, for your own sake. But for now, since you've ruined the party, I'm going upstairs to bed."

Eileen held up her hands, and between them, Paulette and Ronnie managed to hoist her off the sofa and propel her toward the vestibule. They made it to the upstairs landing, as far as the studio door before Eileen shoved them aside.

"I'd appreciate some privacy," she said.

Ronnie cast an inquiring glance at Paulette, who sighed and told her mother she would see her in the morning.

"Holler if you need anything," said Ronnie.

Eileen stumbled into the studio and hastily slammed the door.

"She won't ask for help," Paulette observed. "Not if her life depends on it. She hates anyone to see her at anything less than her best."

"Drunk or sober, she's quite a lady. She's certainly been a lifesaver to me."

"How do you mean?"

"She's offered to fill in while my pianist's out with the flu. Of course, she claims she's not very good."

"Don't you believe it. She plays the piano beautifully, just like she does everything else."

"Don't be too hard on her," Ronnie counseled.

Paulette sighed again, more deeply. "Have you any idea how strange it feels to see her, not as my mother, but as a *person*?"

Ronnie grinned. "It happens to all of us sooner or later. Welcome to the real world, Paulette."

EILEEN WENT TO EARLY SERVICES that Sunday. Although it seemed unlikely that Paulette would miss her, she left a note explaining her whereabouts.

"Back by nine," she wrote. "We'll have breakfast, and afterward we'll take care of your Jacuzzi and massage."

Paulette heard the street door close when her mother left the building. A few minutes later she found the note, but she didn't wait for her bath.

In the real world, adults did not overdramatize their injuries, so she managed the whirlpool by herself. Getting dressed presented minor difficulties, but she managed that as well, and by the time her mother walked in, she had prepared orange juice and sausages and was pouring some pancake batter onto the griddle.

Eileen surveyed the breakfast table with visible dismay. "Sorry I'm late," she said. "Father Walsh is so long-winded. Can I help with anything?"

"You can pour the coffee," Paulette replied. "The pot's hard for me to handle when it's full. I had to fill the coffee maker in stages."

"Even so, you seem to have made a miraculous recovery."

"I'm working on it."

Paulette transferred the pancakes to plates, which her mother carried to the table. As they seated themselves, Eileen remarked, "You're not wearing your collar. Should I take it as a hint that you're tired of my company?"

"No, Mother. What makes you think that?"

"Well, after last night—"

"Last night I behaved like a spoiled brat."

"You won't get any argument from me about that, but my behavior wasn't much better."

"To err is human, Mother."

Eileen responded with a pained smile. "The way my head ached when I woke up this morning, I'd say a little too human."

"I'm sorry you have a hangover," said Paulette.

"Don't be. I consider it penance."

"Penance or not, I hope you took something for it."

"As a matter of fact, I helped myself to one of your pain pills. That's the only way I could make it to church."

"Then it helped?"

"Oh, yes. My headache's gone, but I'm not sure I can face these pancakes." Eileen prodded the edge of one with the tines of her fork. "Do they seem a bit heavy to you?"

They didn't. Not at all. The pancakes were done to a delicate golden brown, and they tasted as good as they looked. Paulette thought they had a fine, light consistency, and she realized this was one more instance of her mother finding fault. But today, instead of counterattacking, she turned the other cheek.

"If you don't like the pancakes, don't eat them," she said, "but whenever you feel up to it, I think we should have a talk."

Eileen laid her fork across her plate. "That sounds ominous."

"It's not meant to. It's just that I'd like us to be closer."

"I'd like that too, only I'm supposed to meet Ronnie at the rehearsal hall at ten." Eileen dabbed at her lips with her napkin and pushed away from the table. "I gave her my word, dear. I hope you understand. Oh, and don't bother with the dishes. I'll do them when I get back."

She was gone before Paulette could reply, and perhaps that was just as well.

When duty called, her mother answered, regardless of the occasion. It never seemed to occur to her that her daughter might appreciate some of the devotion she gave to others.

Paulette understood this. She understood it perfectly, and she knew that if she had objected, if she had admitted how much she needed a confidante, her mother might have stayed. But knowing this didn't make her disappointment easier to bear.

She was still fuming about her mother's defection when Jonathan called at noon.

"Like mother, like daughter," he said.

"Are you saying I'm elusive?"

"Are fish slippery?"

Paulette didn't like being subjected to her own tactics. "What do fish have to do with anything?"

"Think about it," Jonathan replied. "Think what happens when you tempt a fish with the right bait, the right hook."

Paulette had never done much fishing. She didn't have the temperament for it. But when she was four or five her parents had given her a goldfish. She remembered feeding Goldie "no more than a pinch," and cleaning the fish tank, just as her mother had taught her. But Goldie had survived less than a month.

Paulette had wept the morning she discovered her pet, floating belly-up at the top of the aquarium, and she remembered running to her father, crawling onto his lap, wailing that she had taken good care of Goldie.

"Of course you did," her father said.

"Then why'd she have to die?"

"I don't know, polliwog."

Until then her father had answered all her questions. She had thought he always would. She'd stared at him, openmouthed, sliding off his knee.

"It's not fair!" she'd cried.

Her father hadn't disagreed. He'd simply dried her tears and asked if she'd like to give Goldie a funeral.

With his help she had found a Band-Aid tin to use as a coffin, and together they had buried the goldfish in the backyard, beneath a lilac bush. They knelt by the grave and offered a prayer, and on the way back to the house her father took her hand.

"You loved Goldie, baby. She brought you joy. But no matter how much we care or how good our intentions, our earthly life is short." He'd smiled and wiped a smudge of dirt from her cheek. "That's one thing we cannot change."

In the twenty-five years since Goldie's death, Paulette had identified a few more of life's constants. One was taxes. Another was her parents.

Her father's hair had thinned. His shoulders were stooped and he wore bifocals now, but at heart he was the same sweet-tempered, absentminded man he'd been when she was five.

And until last night she had believed her mother hadn't changed, either. But now she wasn't sure, so she sat in Jonathan's living room thinking about bait and hooks, waiting for her mother to return.

PAULETTE HAD JUST TURNED on the TV when Eileen finally got home.

"How was rehearsal?"

"Wonderful! I don't know when I've had a more exhilarating four hours. Ronnie is an extraordinary young lady."

"She must be very talented to inspire your praise." Paulette made an effort to match her mother's enthusiasm, but even to her own ears the response didn't sound convincing. She cleared her throat and tried again, striving for more warmth and less envy. "Will you be accompanying her again?"

"Mm-hmm. We've made definite plans for rehearsals tomorrow and Tuesday. After that, if you'll excuse the pun, we'll have to play it by ear."

"I'm glad you enjoyed yourself, Mother." *That's better,* Paulette thought. At least it sounded sincere.

After hanging her coat in the guest closet, Eileen vanished into the kitchen. If she noticed that Paulette had taken care of the breakfast dishes, she made no comment.

"There's some soup on the stove for lunch," Paulette called.

"Thanks anyway, but Ronnie and I stopped for a sandwich after we finished. I could use some tea, though. How about you?"

"That would be nice."

Paulette stared at the television without registering the action on the screen while Eileen filled the kettle and made a pot of tea. The moment she came into the living room, Paulette reached for the remote control.

"Don't turn it off," said Eileen. "I don't want to interrupt your movie."

"That's all right. I've already seen it."

Eileen poured tea for Paulette and stirred sugar into her own cup. "Tell me about your day, dear. Did Jonathan call?"

Paulette nodded.

"Why the long face? Did you have a quarrel?"

"Not really. It's just that Jack said something that reminded me of Goldie. Do you remember her?"

"Indeed I do," Eileen replied brusquely. "As I recall, one of your friends got an aquarium for her birthday, and nothing would do but that you have one too. You pouted for days until your father caved in and bought you that goldfish, then you lost interest in her within a week."

Paulette frowned and rubbed her forehead. "I don't remember any of that."

"It's no wonder. You were much too young." Eileen kicked off her shoes and settled back in her chair. "Now

I have one for you. Do you remember the time I took you to the circus?"

"Of course I do." Surprised by a wave of nostalgia, Paulette recalled the clowns, the jugglers, the high wire act, but once again there was a wide divergence between her mother's memory and her own.

With a mock shudder, Eileen recalled, "I didn't see the show because you wandered off in the crowd. I don't mind telling you I was petrified. I thought I'd never find you. And that wasn't the first time you pulled your disappearing act."

"It wasn't?"

"Goodness, no! You were always running off. Why, even when you were learning to walk, you'd never let me hold your hand, and as soon as you were steady on your feet, you started exploring, testing the boundaries—"

"Sometimes trampling on them?" Paulette suggested.

"Sometimes," Eileen agreed. "And I'd have to punish you."

"I remember being sent to my room a lot, but I don't remember what I did to deserve it."

"That's unfortunate, dear, but I suppose it's not unusual. The truth is, I hated being the disciplinarian. I used to worry about hampering your independence, but from your point of view, I must have seemed like an ogre."

Paulette shook her head. "I wouldn't put it that strongly."

"How would you put it?"

"Let's just say that you commanded my respect."

"What about your affection?"

"What about yours, Mother?"

Eileen fumbled with the collar on her blouse. "I've never been very demonstrative, so you might not believe me, but I loved you, dear—"

"Then why were you so strict?"

"Because you gave me no choice! You'd do things right in front of me. There was no way I could ignore them."

"I was a child, Mother. Children misbehave. They aren't perfect."

Eileen drew herself taller. "Neither are parents."

Paulette caught her lower lip between her teeth. Her mouth was dry, her bravado exhausted. Was it possible she had made the mistake of applying her mother's standard of perfection to her parents? If so, perhaps the time had come to admit her own culpability and let bygones be bygones.

"I guess I didn't set the best example for Nicole," she said.

"Yes, well, it's hard being the oldest child. Almost as hard as being a mother."

Eileen's tone was astringent, but her smile offered absolution. She poured another round of tea, and as she and Paulette compared reminiscences in the early winter twilight, it became obvious that she was aware of Nicole's pending divorce.

"No thanks to your sister," Eileen said.

"How did you find out?"

"I assure you, it wasn't difficult. When Dad and I phoned at Christmas, all the children talked about was this Eddie person, so I put two and two together and figured out that Nicole's tagged him as husband number four."

Paulette swirled the tea leaves at the bottom of her cup. "I'm sorry you had to hear the news that way."

"I'm sorry too. Sorry that Nicole feels she can't share her problems with me. I'd always thought when you girls grew up, the three of us would be friends."

Paulette set her cup on the tray and touched Eileen's hand. "Don't give up on us, Mother. It could still happen."

Chapter Sixteen

Jonathan had dinner with Dina Zhenkov that Sunday. When Dina phoned, she said she wanted to discuss business, so he suggested they meet at a restaurant near his motel.

"Let's make it The Rafters," she said. "It's just off the Pacific Coast Highway—"

"Yes, I know the place."

"Very well, then. Eight o'clock?"

"Eight's fine," he agreed.

Since he'd missed his morning jog, he decided to walk to the restaurant. Although it was early, he had the sidewalk to himself, which seemed to confirm the rumor that Angelenos never walked if they could drive.

He arrived at The Rafters ten minutes before eight, but Dina was already waiting. She was an acknowledged beauty, stylish and smart, but she couldn't hold a candle to Paulette. Paulette, he thought, was more spontaneous, more vibrant, more alive.

"Where's your topcoat?" Dina inquired, slipping her mink-lined bomber jacket off her shoulders.

"Back in my room. It's a pleasant night."

"Pleasant! My God, Jon, it's in the forties."

"That's warm compared to Madison."

"It's too warm for furs, too, but that doesn't keep the women out here from wearing them."

"I've noticed," he said.

Dina gave the coat-check girl custody of her jacket, and linked arms with him as they followed the maître d' to their table. While Jonathan conferred with the waiter and the wine steward, she fitted an unfiltered cigarette into a long ebony holder. He held a match for her, and she steadied his hand with hers, studying him through the flame. When the cigarette was lighted, she tipped her head back so that her sleek pageboy spilled like black ink along the paleness of her neck.

Like many of her gestures, this one struck Jonathan as studied. It occurred to him that Sergei was not the only Zhenkov who rehearsed in front of mirrors, and he settled back in his chair, preparing to enjoy the performance.

Dina blew a plume of smoke toward the chandelier and focused the considerable power of her charm on him. "One thing I admire about you, Jon. You're one of those rare men who doesn't treat an innocent meeting as if it were an assignation."

"I'm flattered, Dina, but you did say something about business."

"Ah, but that might have been a ploy. I like it that you don't assume I'm making a pass."

Jonathan smiled. "If you were making a pass, I'm sure you wouldn't leave anything to assumption. Besides, we both know that, beneath that fancy whatchamacallit you're wearing, your heart belongs to Sergei."

Dina laughed and touched one carmine-tipped finger to the pin on her lapel. "This whatchamacallit happens to be a diamond and emerald chameleon from Cartier."

"I'll take your word for it," said Jonathan. "You're the fashion expert."

"Yes, I am. I'm the best damned costume designer this side of the Atlantic, which brings up the topic I wanted to talk to you about."

Dina stubbed out her cigarette, suddenly intent. Over the consommé, she recited her credentials, from her undergraduate studies on both sides of the Atlantic to her apprenticeship in summer stock and civic repertory work.

Over the salad she talked about her credits: a season with the Icecapades, another with a major opera company, and then her move to Hollywood.

"That's when I met Sergei," she said. "I was the assistant costume designer for his first film."

Over the chateaubriand she did some name-dropping. "To demonstrate I've made contacts," she explained. "Thanks to my husband, I have influential friends in Hollywood and New York."

When the dessert cart arrived, she said, "You're probably wondering why I'm telling you all this."

"I assume you're establishing your qualifications," said Jonathan. "Are you thinking of branching into some related business?"

Dina attacked her chocolate mousse. "Women's fashions," she declared. "I want to become the next Gloria Vanderbilt."

"So you're looking for investors."

"Also guidance. I have the talent, the training and the experience to handle the creative end, but I want to avoid financial pitfalls."

"How does Sergei feel about this venture?"

"He's been very supportive. He's agreed to back me, if you approve."

"And if I don't?"

"I'll find backers elsewhere." The waiter approached with their coffee, and Dina was silent till he'd finished serving. "Listen, Jon, I realize you represent Sergei. We'd prefer to keep this in the family, but we're prepared to abide by your decision."

"Have you worked up some sort of proposal?"

"I have a preliminary estimate of start-up costs." Dina opened her shoulder bag and removed a thick manila envelope. "I've done my homework, Jon. I think you'll find the figures are fairly complete."

"I'll look them over and get back to you," said Jonathan, accepting the envelope. "If the deal's not right for Sergei, perhaps I can help you arrange alternative financing."

"I was hoping you'd say that. Any advice you can give me will be welcome, but of course I know how valuable your time is. I expect to reimburse you for this."

He shook his head. "This is more or less in the line of duty. If my recommendation isn't favorable, we'll chalk it up to professional courtesy."

The waiter appeared with their bill, and Jonathan gave Dina ten points for perfect timing.

They were outside the restaurant, window-shopping at an adjoining store while they waited for the parking attendant to bring Dina's car around, when Jonathan spotted the doll.

He moved closer to the window, then sat on his heels so that he could study the doll at eye level.

She was rather bedraggled. The faded color in her cheeks gave her a vaguely consumptive appearance. She'd lost one shoe, and her blue pinafore had seen better days. But she had a brown ponytail and eyes that opened and shut and a brave painted smile that would melt the heart of any seven-year-old girl.

Dina strolled up beside him and peered at the doll. "Why, that's Chatty Cathy! I had a doll exactly like that when I was ten."

"I wonder if she still talks," said Jonathan.

"It'd be a miracle if she did. Poor thing. She looks so sad. She's really been through the mill."

Jonathan rose and started toward the door of the shop. "I'm going to buy her."

Dina caught hold of his arm. "The store's not open."

"Then I'll come back tomorrow."

"But she's terribly shabby, Jon. I think most little girls would rather have a new doll."

"She's not for a little girl. She's for a big one."

"A girl about your size?"

"Closer to yours, but she's just right for me."

During the drive to his motel, Dina quizzed him about Paulette. She asked "How long have you known her?" and "How did you meet?" and "What sort of work does she do?" She asked him to describe Paulette, but once he got beyond red hair and gray-green eyes he found himself at a loss.

"She's kind of hard to pin down," he said. It seemed easier to deal with abstractions, and so he talked about the significance of Chatty Cathy. He spoke of dreams and disillusionment, and when Dina pulled off the highway, she said, "I'd like to meet this woman, Jon. I think we have a lot in common."

"Yes," he replied. "In some ways you remind me of her."

"It's an odd coincidence, isn't it?"

"What is?"

"Well, Paulette tells you that story, and then we happen to meet in that particular restaurant at the very time Chatty Cathy's on display in the store window." Dina parked the car beneath the motel's portico, and turned to him. "I do have one suggestion, though. I wish you'd let me spruce up the doll before you give her to Paulette. I have a friend who's a genius at restoring toys, and I could make a new outfit for her."

"It's nice of you to offer, but—"

"I won't take no for an answer, Jon. If you won't charge me for your time, at least let me do this."

Jonathan gathered up the manila envelope. "Well, if you're sure you don't mind, I'd appreciate it."

"Shall I meet you at the store, then?"

"Sure," he said, climbing out of the car. "About ten tomorrow morning?"

"Great! And I promise I'll take good care of Chatty Cathy. I'll fix her up and deliver her to you by the end of next week."

"I'll be working in the Bay Area by then."

"There's another coincidence! Sergei's scheduled to do a benefit in San Francisco, so we're driving up the coast on Saturday. If you let us know where you're staying, we can drop the doll on our way. But maybe you should wait and give her to Paulette for Valentine's Day. If we're as much alike as I suspect, it doesn't pay to rush her." Dina laughed and drew her mink-lined jacket closer about her shoulders. "Isn't it funny, Jon? It's almost like fate."

AT NOON ON MONDAY, Anne Gallagher stopped by with the scholarship committee files and a get-well-quick message from Carl Bemis.

"I think he's afraid you won't be back on the job for registration week," Anne told Paulette.

"I'll be there," said Paulette. "Tell Carl he can count on me."

"When does registration start?" Eileen asked.

"Not till next Monday," Paulette answered firmly, anticipating her mother's protest, but Eileen only shrugged and suggested Paulette get her doctor's approval before she returned to work.

"There's been a dramatic improvement since Saturday," Eileen informed Anne. The conspiratorial look they exchanged was not lost on Paulette.

"You two are up to something," she said, "and I want to know what it is."

"It's nothing sinister," said Eileen. "We were merely concerned about you."

Anne patted the stack of file folders on the coffee table. "Your mother thought you seemed depressed, so we decided work might be therapeutic."

"Not a bad prescription," Paulette murmured. Work was not a panacea, but it might give her the strength to put the interlude with Jonathan behind her and get on with her life.

She didn't mention Jonathan, however, and as if by unspoken agreement, neither did Anne or her mother.

Instead, Eileen invited Anne to stay for lunch. "It won't be fancy," she said. "We had some chicken left over from dinner last night, so I'm fixing chicken salad."

"Sounds delicious," Anne replied. "Can I help with anything?"

"No, thanks. I can manage."

Eileen excused herself and hurried toward the kitchen, and Paulette glanced quizzically at Anne.

"Is this supposed to be my cue to confide in you?"

"Only if you want to, Paulette. You know I'd never pry."

"I appreciate that, Annie, and I owe you one for going out of your way to bring me the files, but if it's all the same to you, I'd rather not talk about Jack."

"You've got it. Only I wish I understood why you're so blasted sure there's no future for you and Jonathan."

"I told you before, if you met him you'd know why."

"Nonsense!" Eileen stepped into the dining alcove, a bread knife in one hand. "I've met Jonathan and I haven't an inkling what you're talking about."

"Oh, Mother, don't hand me that! You must've noticed how responsible he is."

"What's wrong with being responsible? I should think you'd consider it a virtue."

"I do, but—"

"There you are then!" Eileen brandished the knife as if the matter were resolved. "You love Jonathan; he loves you—"

"But he doesn't *know* me. Can't you see? Jack's in love with a Paulette who doesn't exist. She's a figment of his imagination who happens to look like me. She's as responsible as he is. She's capable of making commitments and meeting them. If he really got to know me, he'd be disappointed."

"For heaven's sake, Paulette. Whatever gave you that idea? You've been a daughter all your life and a sister almost that long. You've worked at Shorewood for seven years, and you and Anne have been friends for five. In my book, that's not a bad track record for someone who claims she can't make commitments."

"Right on!" Anne cheered. "As for responsibility, everyone at Shorewood knows your boss is just putting in his time till he retires. In everything but name and salary, you've been the registrar for the last two years, and you've been a darned good one. You can't pass a Salvation Army kettle without dropping in a donation. You can't pass a nursing home without stopping to cheer up the shut-ins—"

"But I enjoy doing those things," Paulette argued.

"Naturally you do," said Eileen. "But the fact that you enjoy them doesn't make them any less responsible."

Paulette's gaze shifted from her mother to Anne, then back to her mother again. There was an appealing logic in their pep talk. Never mind that her mother's caustic delivery made compliments seem critical, or that Anne's generosity could make criticism seem complimentary. Never mind that both of them were biased, or that their descriptions made her sound too good to be true—like Florence Nightingale played by one of Charlie's Angels.

"I want to believe you," she said.

"Why wouldn't you?" Eileen huffed. "I'm not in the habit of lying."

Anne held out one hand, palm upturned in supplication. "Will you at least think about what we've said?"

On a note of rising hope, Paulette promised that she would.

AT A CARNIVAL the summer before she started school, Paulette had sneaked into the fun house. For half an hour or more, surrounded by banks of mirrors, she confronted reflections of herself, each more grotesque than the one before.

She saw herself alternately shrunken and expanded, with an elongated head, rubbery features, stubby arms and legs, a body like Humpty-Dumpty's, and when she found her way out of the maze, she was terrified that the distortions would be permanent.

For days afterward she had avoided mirrors, and then one afternoon, at the supermarket with her mother, she caught a glimpse of a little girl in the store window. She had stopped for a closer look, and recognized herself. She'd stared at this reassuring image for a long time, wondering how other people saw her.

Did they see a pigtailed five-year-old, or the monster from the fun house mirrors?

At five her attention span was limited. She was easily diverted. A week later she'd started kindergarten, and the fun house incident had remained buried in her subconscious until the issues raised by Anne and her mother resurrected it.

For the next few days Paulette tried to reconcile the woman they had described with the way she saw herself, and the more she questioned her own perceptions, the more confused she became.

Which was the real Paulette? she wondered, and which the distortion? Was she mature and responsible, capable of sustaining a forever kind of relationship, or was she the good-time girl who didn't believe in love?

There were moments when she felt as if she had fallen through a time warp into a maze of mirrors from which there was no escape. And this time, she realized, she would not find the answers to her questions reflected in a store window.

On Friday she saw her doctor. He okayed her return to work, and at dinner that evening, Eileen announced she was leaving the next morning.

"You know how your father is," she told Paulette. "He's so busy looking after his parishioners, he forgets to take care of himself. Besides, I miss him. In thirty-three years of marriage, this is the longest we've been apart."

"Thirty-three years, and never a cross word between you," Paulette marveled. "That's quite an achievement."

"It would be a remarkable feat if it were true."

"But it *is* true, Mother. At least, I've never heard you and Dad fight."

"That doesn't mean we haven't had our disagreements. Believe me, dear, some of them were dillies. But we've always been careful to keep them to ourselves. When we were first married, your father and I thought it was important to maintain an image for the sake of his ministry, and after you and Nicole came along, we tried to present a united front for your sakes, so that you wouldn't feel insecure."

Eileen tipped her head to one side, as if she were listening to distant echoes of long-forgotten battles. A V-shaped furrow appeared between her eyebrows as she went on. "At the time it made sense, but lately I've wondered if we did you girls a disservice."

"What kind of disservice?"

"We created a false impression. You see, dear, marriage is a labor of love, and a good deal of the time, the emphasis is on the labor. But that only makes the love more precious. Couples have problems. They work them out, and in the process they draw closer. But Nicole's not willing to work her way through the downside of marriage. She has this harebrained notion that the sea of matrimony should always be smooth sailing.

At the first sign of a storm she abandons ship. And as for you, Paulette, you won't even get in the boat."

"Maybe I'm afraid of the water, Mother, but not everyone's cut out to be a sailor. Is there anything wrong with that?"

"Not if you're happy with the status quo."

Eileen's reply was as bland as her smile. She didn't actually accuse Paulette of cowardice, but she didn't have to. Paulette was capable of providing the accusation herself.

Jonathan's apartment seemed unnaturally quiet after her mother left. Paulette wandered from room to room, and everywhere she looked she saw reminders of what might have been.

By midafternoon on Saturday she had gathered her belongings and moved upstairs to the studio, but memories hounded her even there. The hours till Monday stretched before her, empty and endless.

She spent the rest of that day, and most of the night, thinking about her parents and Nicole, about marriage and divorce, success and failure, and by Sunday morning, ready for diversion, she tuned in *That Touch of Mink* on one of the cable channels.

She had seen the movie several times, but Cary Grant's efforts to seduce Doris Day had never failed to amuse her, and that day was no exception.

When Doris broke out in a rash rather than go to bed with Cary, Paulette sympathized, and when Doris returned to the scene of her humiliation, determined to show Cary that a freckle-faced Midwesterner could be as sophisticated as the jet set ladies he knew, Paulette applauded.

Near the end of the movie, the prospect of marriage made Cary break out in a rash, and when a serene, starry-eyed Doris assured him everything would be all right, Paulette believed her.

Cary, however, was dubious. His hang-up was love; Doris's lovemaking. How would they resolve their differences?

"You don't know the girls from Sandusky," Doris told him, and with the swiftness of cinematic magic, his faith was restored.

The closing scene showed Doris and Cary as proud parents, wheeling their daughter's carriage along a New York City street, which proved they would live happily ever after.

While the credits rolled, Paulette found herself wishing that real life were as simple as the movies.

She ate lunch and did some laundry, and wondered what Doris Day would do in her situation.

As the afternoon waned she thought about love, and inevitably her thoughts turned toward Jonathan.

In the four weeks since they'd met, they'd had only ten days together. But she knew with a certainty that defied reason that he had become essential to her. She could not give him up. Not without a fight. She had made it through the weekend—barely. But without him, how could she make it through the rest of her life?

Chapter Seventeen

Twenty-four hours later at the Shorewood campus, Anne stopped by the registrar's office on her way home from work. She had just come from supervising the English department's registration table in the gymnasium, and the hubbub and confusion and long lines of students had taken their toll, but her face lit up when she saw Paulette.

"You look great!" she said. "Just like your old self."

Paulette spread her arms wide, as if she would embrace the world. "I feel great, Annie. It's as if this awful weight has been taken from me. I feel lighter than air, and I owe it all to you and my mother."

"Does this mean you've reached a decision about Jonathan?"

"Are dimes thin?"

"Don't keep me in suspense. What did you decide?"

Paulette smiled. "I'm going to move in with him."

"I knew it! I just knew it!" Anne flew at Paulette and gave her a quick hug. Both of them were laughing. "I'm so happy for you, Paulette. And your mother must be thrilled."

"She'd be more pleased if I were announcing my engagement, but I haven't told her yet. I haven't even told Jack."

Anne sobered. "What are you waiting for?"

"Give me a break, Annie. I only made up my mind last night, and this is the kind of thing I'd rather discuss in person."

"Yes, yes. I understand. But when is Jonathan due home?"

"This Saturday. I'm meeting him at the airport at three."

"And after that?"

"That's as far as I've gotten." Paulette propped her elbows on the counter and stared into space, her expression distant and dreamy. "I'd like us to go someplace special. Someplace romantic. I want to give Jack an evening he'll always remember."

"Oh, God, this is so exciting!"

"I hope so, Annie. Do you have any suggestions?"

"Not off the top of my head." Anne gripped the ends of her muffler and slid it back and forth beneath her coat collar. "What does Jonathan particularly enjoy?"

"Well, he likes chess. But that's too cerebral. And skiing's too athletic. And tobogganing's out because of the weather."

"Right," said Anne. An Arctic cold front had gripped the upper Midwest, and with the windchill hovering at thirty below, it was dangerous to be outdoors.

"There's basketball," Paulette continued. "The Badgers are playing Iowa. I could take him to the game."

Anne plucked at a loose thread on her muffler. "You wouldn't have much privacy, surrounded by thousands of fans."

Paulette frowned. "I guess that rules out movies, plays and concerts."

"Yes, it does, but you could always go out to dinner."

"Too ordinary," said Paulette.

Anne gave the thread an absent tug, unraveling a row of stitches. "If this were summer you could go canoeing on Lake Mendota. You could have a picnic on the beach, and go for a moonlight swim—"

"Wait a minute, Annie. We don't have to stay in Madison. We could go south for the weekend. We could go to Florida, or even the Bahamas."

"That would be romantic, but awfully expensive. Besides, Jonathan's been on the road so much, he might prefer to stay home."

Paulette cupped her chin in her hand. The logistics of Saturday night were turning out to be much more complicated than she had imagined. "Think, Annie," she said. "Think back to when you and Ben were dating. What were the most romantic things you did?"

Anne wound the thread around her finger, and the fringe on her muffler widened. "We never did anything terribly spectacular, Paulette. We went for walks in the arboretum and bicycled around the lake. We used to sit on the terrace at the students' union and watch the sailboats and listen to bluegrass and jazz. On our first date Ben took me to the opera, and afterward we had a late supper at the Edgewater. We went to parties and visited friends, but the most satisfying times were the times we spent alone, just the two of us, whether we were at Ben's place, or mine, or in the back seat of his car."

"The back of his car? Surely you jest."

Anne looked smug. "If you haven't tried it, don't knock it. When you love someone, where you are isn't nearly as important as who you're with. What matters is being together."

A silence ensued, during which Anne unraveled more of her muffler and Paulette's chin sank deeper into her palm. At last she said, "Maybe I should fix dinner at my place."

Anne nodded. "If Jack's anything like Ben, that might be the best idea yet."

PAULETTE MADE CAREFUL PLANS for Saturday. She wanted everything to be perfect. She made a list labeled Things to Do, and at the top of the list she wrote, "Look my best."

The last time Jonathan saw her she had been covered with bruises, dazed and dopey and decidedly unalluring, so she had a lot to overcome.

On Tuesday evening, she and Anne went shopping, and as they walked into Marshall Field's, Paulette described what she had in mind.

"I want sparkle, but I don't want glitz. I want natural glamour, feminine chic, domestic refinement. I want to look soft, touchable, gorgeous."

"Is that all?" said Anne.

Paulette stamped the snow off her boots. "It would be nice to find something warm. And it wouldn't hurt if it were on sale."

Anne waved aside the saleslady's offer of assistance and waded into the dress racks herself, muttering "This is a job for Supershopper."

Paulette spent the next two hours in the dressing room trying on the garments Anne located. She tried lounging pajamas, jumpsuits, day dresses and hostess gowns, and one green velvet number that reminded her of a pool table.

"Six ball in the corner pocket," she said.

Anne gave her a harried smile and another armload of selections. "Time's wasting, hotshot. Get yourself into some of these."

Paulette tried on silks and synthetics, chiffons and jacquards. She tried taffeta, linen and lace. She tried a rainbow of knits and bias-cut crepe, and just when it seemed she would have to go home empty-handed, Anne brought in a shimmery peach confection with a flared skirt, figure-hugging bodice and long graceful sleeves, with a garland of golden embroidery across the shoulders.

She studied the effect in the mirror while Anne fastened the last few inches of the back zipper and thought, *This is it. This is exactly what I've been looking for.*

The saleslady poked her head through the curtains to see how they were doing. "Isn't the fabric luscious? Doesn't it have a feeling of understated luxury?"

Paulette agreed that it did, and Anne offered the caveat, "If you want to see conspicuous luxury, take a look at the price tag."

"And worth every penny," the saleslady insisted. "That dress was made for you, my dear. See how beautifully it fits."

Paulette checked the price tag, then took a closer look at the dress. *So what if it's not on sale?* she thought. *It gives me a feeling of confidence.*

Meeting the saleslady's gaze in the mirror, she said, "I'll take it."

In the minutes before the store closed, Paulette found a pair of gold kid sandals to wear with the dress. That cleared the deck for the second item on her agenda: the menu.

On Wednesday afternoon she stopped at the library and chose an assortment of cookbooks. She was reading James Beard that evening when Ronnie dropped by the studio to deliver an invitation to her recital.

"What's up?" Ronnie asked, leafing through a copy of *The French Chef*. "Are you having a party?"

"For two," Paulette answered, and went on to explain her plans for Saturday. "I don't want to spend the whole night in the kitchen," she said, "so I'd like to keep the meal simple. But it shouldn't taste simple."

Ronnie nodded sagely. "Fettuccine Alfredo."

"Feta who?"

"Fettuccine Alfredo." Ronnie touched her fingertips to her lips and tossed a kiss at the ceiling. "It's quick. It's yummy. And best of all, it's easy. All you do is toss fettuccine al dente with heavy cream and butter, add Parmesan cheese, salt and pepper, a dash of nutmeg—"

"Just a minute. I'd better write this down."

Paulette found a paper and pencil, and Ronnie dictated the recipe in detail, adding, "Of course, to do it right you have to use the freshest ingredients, and you'll want to start with homemade pasta."

"I've never made pasta," said Paulette. "Isn't it difficult?"

"It takes a while to knead the dough and roll it out, but you can make your noodles ahead of time, let them dry and store them."

"Don't you need a pasta machine?"

"Nope. Homemade pasta's better than the packaged stuff, but *hand*made is the ultimate."

Paulette chewed on the eraser end of the pencil, wondering if fettuccine Alfredo might be more trouble than it was worth. "What would I serve with it?" she asked.

"Stuffed zucchini's always good. So are marinated mushrooms. Or if you want you could have a salad, and maybe veal scaloppine with marsala."

Paulette's mouth was watering, but still she hesitated.

"What the heck," said Ronnie. "If you'd like me to, I'll help you with the pasta."

Over the next few hours, Paulette discovered that Ronnie's idea of help consisted of expert advice and the loan of a rolling pin. She also learned that kneading pasta dough and rolling it out to Ronnie's exacting specifications required skill, patience and effort.

After she had slaved over the first batch for forty minutes, the dough lost its elasticity and came out lumpy and uneven. Ronnie decreed the mess unfit for human consumption, and Paulette had to start all over again.

By this time she had developed a more adroit touch with the dough, and after another half hour of kneading and pommeling and stretching, she managed to fashion the pasta into an almost paper-thin transparent sheet.

"How's that?" she asked.

"Not bad," said Ronnie. "Not bad at all."

"What's next?"

"You fold it, but first you say a prayer that the dough doesn't crack."

Ronnie bowed her head and steepled her palms while Paulette made the first fold. "So far, so good," she said. Paulette held her breath and kept her touch light and folded the dough into quarters, eighths, sixteenths. Somehow, between the two of them, the sheet of pasta was transformed into a neat rectangular roll.

At ten o'clock Ronnie pronounced the pasta ready for cutting, and by eleven the kitchen was festooned with strands of drying egg noodles.

"They're leathery," Paulette fretted. "Like thongs."

"Don't worry. If they're not fettuccine tomorrow, you can use them to lace your boots."

After Ronnie had taken her rolling pin and gone home, Paulette showered and took one of her pills. The kitchen needed cleaning, but that would have to wait till morning. Her arms felt leaden. Her neck was stiff. She'd had enough of a workout for one day.

She had just climbed into bed when Jonathan called. He said, "Guess who I had dinner with," and without waiting for her response, named a movie star who had recently gone into politics.

"He's the client who's interested in the Kon-Tiki," Jonathan said. "But if the deal goes through, he wants to feature Italian cuisine."

"What did you have for dinner?" asked Paulette.

"Abalone." Jonathan was surprised that she had focused on the food rather than his client, but after faltering for a moment, he inquired, "How was your day?"

"It was okay. The campus is always a madhouse during registration week, but it's nice to be back."

Jonathan hadn't commented on her move to the studio, and she wondered why. She debated telling him about the fettuccine, then chose another topic. "I had lunch with Anne today. She'd like to meet you."

"I'd like to meet her too, but I'm afraid the introductions will have to wait till my work out here is finished."

"Can you estimate when that will be?"

"Barring complications, another five or six weeks ought to do it."

"But you'll be in town this weekend?"

"Wouldn't miss it."

The rough intimacy of Jonathan's voice sent ripples of pleasure through Paulette. The thought that he would interrupt his busy schedule and travel halfway across the country just to spend one night with her made her feel special, desirable, loved. Her own voice was husky as she said, "Where are you now, Jack?"

"About ten miles north of Big Sur. Listen." There was a silence, followed by a faint whooshing sound that rose and fell to a distinct and soothing tempo. "That's the Pacific. Did you hear it? The motel's right on the beach."

Paulette tucked the receiver into the hollow of her shoulder and smoothed one hand over the cool percale pillow slip, remembering the resilient warmth of Jonathan's skin.

"Is the coastline as wonderful as they say?"

"It's fantastic. You'd love it here, Paulette. Someday I want to show it to you."

Someday.

The two short syllables implied so much. They seemed to offer everything she'd ever dreamed of.

Paulette closed her eyes and rubbed her cheek against the pillow, picturing the bold planes and angles of Jonathan's face. *I miss you, Jack Day. I need you. Without you, I'm only half alive.*

She mouthed the words silently, longing to say them aloud. But this was not the time or the place. When she confessed her feelings for Jonathan, she wanted to be in his arms.

JONATHAN CLASPED HIS HANDS behind his head and stared at the ceiling, listening to the surf. As the waves broke against the beach they seemed to say *Don't rush her, don't rush her.* And as they retreated, they whispered *Someday.*

At the foot of the bed, Chatty Cathy sat in her gift box, her head angled toward the window as if she, too, were mesmerized by the waves.

Jonathan swung his feet to the floor and picked up the doll, admiring Dina's handiwork.

"Would you like to play with me?"

Jonathan grinned. The voice was tinny, but the speech mechanism worked. Paulette would be enchanted.

He laid down the doll and picked her up again. Chatty Cathy responded with a rusty "I love you."

"You read my mind," said Jonathan.

God, he was tempted to say those words to Paulette. He wanted to ask her to marry him.

Don't rush her, don't rush her, the ocean sighed.

Jonathan sought a second opinion. "What do you think, Cathy. If I propose this Saturday, will I scare her off?"

The doll gazed at him with glassy eyes, then tumbled onto her back and blinked once for yes.

"That's what I thought," Jonathan muttered.

But the Pacific promised *Someday.*

Chapter Eighteen

By Friday afternoon Paulette had crossed off the last item on her list. The advance preparations were complete. She had tried to foresee every contingency, but still she wasn't satisfied. She went over the list again and again, checking for details she might have overlooked.

"Put the list away," Anne pleaded. "You're the last person I thought I'd say this to, but there is such a thing as overplanning."

Paulette didn't argue, but she didn't put the list away until she had read it one more time.

"I can't help it, Annie," she defended herself. "I have this horrible feeling there's something I've forgotten."

"If there is, it can't be important. You've worn yourself to a frazzle, shopping and cooking and cleaning and—What are you doing?"

Paulette had opened the center drawer of her desk and removed a notepad and pen.

"I'm going to make a new list," she said. "For tomorrow."

Anne snatched the pen as quickly as Paulette uncapped it.

"This isn't like you, Paulette. You've always relied on instinct and luck. I've never seen you this uptight."

"That's because nothing ever meant this much to me." Paulette pressed one hand on the desktop and held the other out to Anne. "Please, give me the pen."

"All right, but as a favor to me, try to relax and enjoy yourself. Trust me, Paulette. Everything's going to work out beautifully."

PAULETTE RECOGNIZED the common sense in Anne's advice, but in an effort to impose order on her chaotic emotions, she went ahead and made out a timetable for Saturday.

She felt better when she had finished, and on the way home, clinging to the overhead handrail on the Metro bus, she imagined how tomorrow would go.

She would meet Jack's flight and they would hurry back to the apartment building—whether to her place or his made no difference, as long as they were together. They would have a blissful reunion, and she would tell him her decision. He would be overjoyed, ecstatic, and if he wanted to tell her he loved her, this time she would listen. They would make a ritual of moving some of her things downstairs to his apartment. He might even carry her over the threshold. And later, toward evening, she would put on her new dress and slip into the kitchen and prepare a feast worthy of a fantasy. She would light the candles. Jack would open the champagne. They would link elbows and toast the future. They would hold hands while they ate, and now and again they would kiss, and their kisses would be sweet and intoxicating, and they would skip dessert because they would not be able to resist each other....

The exit buzzer jarred Paulette from her reverie. She realized she had missed her stop. She scrambled through the knot of passengers in the aisle and made it to the rear door in time to get off at the next corner, and as she began backtracking the six blocks home she thought, *Annie's right. It's silly to worry.*

That night, on the ten o'clock news, the weather girl forecast a warming trend, and Paulette fell asleep secure in the knowledge that fortune had chosen to smile on her. Her plans for tomorrow were foolproof. Even nature seemed inclined to cooperate.

"What could go wrong?" she said to herself. "Everything will go beautifully."

Everything did until just before dawn, when the warming trend brought rain, which froze the instant it left the clouds.

Paulette awoke on Saturday morning to utter stillness and a light so brilliant it hurt her eyes. She squinted out the window into a fairy-tale world of delft-blue skies, spangled rooftops and crystal trees whose branches were crowned with diamonds.

Her first reaction was to marvel at the miracle the ice storm had wrought. The enchantment lasted until she noticed how cold the studio was.

She got out of bed and dragged the comforter with her, wrapping it around herself to ward off the chill. She headed for the thermostat, with a detour past the closet for her slippers.

The thermometer read sixty-two, but the studio felt cooler than that. She flipped the control dial and waited for the heat to come on.

Nothing happened.

She turned the dial higher.

Still nothing.

An icy draft flowed through the register. The metal grating was cold to the touch.

She went to the phone and dialed Ronnie's number. While she waited for the call to go through, she tried the TV. The screen remained blank, and she stared at it, numb with disbelief. Only Ronnie's chirrupy hello kept her from panicking.

"Ronnie," she said, "is your electricity off?"

"Sure is. Isn't this a bummer? Looks like the power's off all over the west side."

"I wonder how long it's going to last?"

"Till evening at least. Madison Gas and Electric has crews out, but a lot of lines are down."

Paulette hauled the comforter closer around her. "Is your apartment as cold as mine?"

"It's cold enough that I wouldn't put my tongue on the pump handle. I'm considering going to a motel. I've been listening to my portable radio, trying to make up my mind."

"Have you heard anything about the airport?"

"It's open, and most of the flights are on schedule."

"So Jack's plane should arrive on time." Paulette's chin quivered. She was torn between hope and despair, and dangerously close to tears.

"Too bad about your dinner party," said Ronnie. "But, hey! Why don't you bundle up in your woollies and come on down and we'll go out for breakfast?"

"Might as well," said Paulette. "There's nothing I can do around here."

NOTHING WENT THE WAY she had planned that day, but once she and Ronnie were seated at the Howard Johnson's near the interstate, Paulette tried to accentuate the positive.

So what if I can't fix dinner? she thought. *It's not my cooking Jack's interested in.*

And later that morning, back in the deep freeze she called home, she pulled on leg warmers and yet another sweater and thought *So what if all these layers of clothing make me look like a bowling pin with feet? Appearances aren't everything.*

And at the airport, when she learned that Jack's flight had been delayed, she thought *So what if he's an hour late? We'll have the whole weekend to make up for it.*

Except that they didn't. But she was happily unaware of how limited their time was until their taxi stopped at the curb in front of the apartment building and Jonathan asked the driver to wait.

"What do you mean, you're not staying?" Paulette sputtered. "I thought you were spending the evening with me."

"I wish I could," said Jonathan, "but there's a meeting I have to go to—"

Paulette had heard enough. With an abruptness that didn't begin to express her indignation, she spun on her heels and marched toward the porch.

Jonathan grabbed his flight bag and hurried after her. "This is something I can't get out of—"

A handful of snow caught him squarely in the face. He stopped in midstride and dragged his hand across his eyes, wondering what had triggered the assault.

Where was the Paulette who'd met his plane? Where was the woman who had run into his arms and welcomed him with kisses? Why had this hellion taken her place?

After a self-conscious glance at the cabdriver, Jonathan dropped his satchel and took a wary step in her direction. "Look, I know you're disappointed—"

Paulette scooped a chunk of snow off the newel post, whirled and fired. Jonathan deflected this missile with his forearm and continued his approach.

"Let's be adult about this, Paulette. Try to understand—"

"You're the one who doesn't understand. I spent most of last week getting ready for tonight. I was going to cook a gourmet dinner for you. I even made pasta. *Handmade* pasta, Jack! Have you any idea how long that takes?"

"I'm sorry you went to all that trouble, but how was I to know? You never mentioned dinner."

"And you never mentioned your meeting."

Paulette's voice had risen to an angry wail. She plunged both hands into the snowbank by the steps, but before she could mount another attack Jonathan bounded onto the porch, clamped his arms about her and propelled her into the vestibule.

"Let me go!"

"Not till you calm down." Jonathan closed the street door with his foot. She tried to wriggle free, and his hold on her tightened. "Please, honey, if you'll give me a chance, I can explain."

The endearment defused her anger. She stopped struggling, but the moment he released her, she backed away from him.

"This'd better be good."

"It is, Paulette. Swear to God. It has to do with Helping Hands."

"The farm relief group?"

"That's right," said Jonathan. "About a year ago, when the Madison chapter was established, the coordinator of their financial planning and relocation assistance program contacted me and asked if I'd be willing to act as a consultant, so I've been working with a couple of local families, doing some counseling."

"That's big of you, Jack, but what does it have to do with tonight?"

"Well, you see, Helping Hands has its own financial difficulties. They've received contributions from FarmAid and a few private donors, but it's been a battle staying solvent, which makes it hard to plan ahead. Part of the problem is public awareness, and part of it is the group has no regular source of income. So last November, the executive committee came up with an idea for a fund-raiser that would help defray administrative costs and give them some good PR. A bachelor auction—"

"A what?"

"A bachelor auction. What it amounts to is rounding up some eligible men and selling a date with each of them to the highest bidder."

"And you're one of the eligibles?"

Jonathan nodded. "The auction's at the Sheraton, the Saturday before Valentine's Day—"

"How appropriate."

"And tonight's our organizational meeting. We're getting together to decide what kind of dates we'll offer and launch the publicity campaign."

"Sounds like they're planning quite a gala."

"I wanted to tell you about it," Jonathan said. "In fact, I tried to tell you once or twice. But I was embarrassed."

"I should think you would be," said Paulette. "If I were you, I'd feel like an idiot, strutting my stuff in front of a mob of leering women."

Jonathan thrust out his chin and swallowed as if his collar were too tight. "The strutting doesn't bother me as much as the price I'll bring."

"If you're concerned about the bidding, why don't you call the people in charge of the auction and tell them you've changed your mind?"

"I can't do that, Paulette. I can't go back on my word."

"I appreciate your integrity, Jack, but if you have to do your bit, how about making a cash donation?"

"That's checkbook charity. If all the bachelors were to back out, there wouldn't be an auction, and without an auction there'd be no ticket sales and no publicity."

"Then what you need is a replacement," said Paulette. "I could find a substitute for you."

"Just like that, I suppose." Jonathan snapped his fingers beneath her nose. His scowl made it clear that he liked this solution even less than the others she had come up with.

"Well, perhaps not that simply—"

"But you do know a lot of bachelors."

"Not in the biblical sense, but yes, I've dated my share."

"You assume we're interchangeable, don't you? We're just fodder for your address book. You reduce men to the lowest common denominator, and make no distinction between the jokers in the pack and a guy who really cares for you. But there is a difference. If you think otherwise, I'd suggest you invite one of your jocks to have dinner with you tonight. I have no doubt you'll find a playmate for the evening, but let me tell you, sweetheart, you'll never find a substitute for me."

Chapter Nineteen

It was the fun house mirror all over again. And this time Paulette identified the monster.

Pride.

Wounded pride that made Jonathan say hateful things to her. Stubborn pride that made her react to his verbal assault with silence.

She didn't say anything, even when Jonathan walked out the door and got into the waiting taxi. The misunderstanding was as much his fault as hers. She was not about to apologize, nor would she dignify his charges with a response.

She spent that night at the Motel Six with Ronnie. She could have gone to the Gallaghers, but Anne would ask too many questions. Questions Paulette was not prepared to answer. All Ronnie expected was a fifty-fifty split of the bill.

By Sunday afternoon M. G. and E. had repaired the lines serving University Heights. Jonathan's car was parked in the driveway when Paulette and Ronnie got home.

"Looks like new," Ronnie remarked. "Smitty's did a good job."

Paulette made no comment. She slammed the street door on her way into the building. She stomped through the vestibule and tarried outside Ronnie's apartment, hoping Jonathan would appear, but she saw no sign of him.

For the rest of that day, closeted in the studio, she tried to come up with a face-saving way of effecting a reconciliation. At nightfall, Jonathan's car was still in the driveway, and she realized he must have taken the morning flight.

By now, she thought, *he must be in California. He didn't wait to say goodbye. It's over. It's really over.*

It suddenly seemed crucial to get rid of the evidence that she had ever dreamed of anything else.

She erased his name from her address book and consigned her expensive new dress to the back of the closet, then gathered up the canister of handmade fettuccine and took it downstairs to Ronnie's. The instant her neighbor opened the door, Paulette shoved the can at her.

"Here," she said. "I won't be needing this."

She ran up the stairs without waiting to be thanked, and Ronnie called after her, "You don't have to use them right away. They'll keep at least a month."

"Maybe they will, but I won't."

Jonathan was gone, and all she had left was her pride.

Before she went to bed that night, Paulette wrote a letter to RentFinders, notifying the leasing agent of her intention to vacate the studio as of March 31. She mailed the letter on her way to Shorewood the next morning, and considered her bridges burned.

That night she worked late, unsnarling the scheduling mix-ups that came with a new semester. She didn't get home till after ten, and as soon as she let herself into the studio, she took the phone off the hook.

If Jonathan called, what could she say to him? And if he didn't call, ignorance was bliss.

With the phone out of commission and the registrar's office so busy, Paulette managed to stay out of Anne's way until Friday. She was in the cafeteria, just finishing lunch when her friend accosted her.

"You've done it again," Anne declared.

"Done what?"

"Pulled your disappearing act. Unplugged your phone. Avoided your friends." Anne dumped her tray on the table with a dish-rattling thump. "Don't bother denying it. I know it's deliberate."

"You're angry," said Paulette.

"Mad as hell."

"I don't blame you. I'm surprised you're speaking to me."

"Frankly, so am I. But we go back a long way. We've been through a lot together, and whether you like it or not, you're stuck with me."

"Why wouldn't I like it?"

"Maybe because friendship entails privileges and risks. I think you're afraid, if I get too close, I'll find out what a phony you really are."

"Thanks, Annie. I love you, too."

"Did you ever try saying that to Jonathan?" Anne unfolded her napkin and spread it across her lap. "I talked to him last night, Paulette. He's been trying to reach you all week, and he's frantic with worry because you won't answer your phone. He told me you'd quarreled—"

"Did he tell you why?"

"No, but I got the impression you were spoiling for a fight."

"I might've started it, but he finished it."

Anne reached for the saltshaker. "He loves you, you know."

"Well, he has a funny way of showing it. He walked out on me, Annie. Stood me up. He chose a committee meeting over me."

"And what did you choose?"

Paulette fidgeted with her dessert spoon, watching her topsy-turvy reflection lift its chin to a haughty angle. "I chose not to have friends second-guess me. I chose not to listen to the latest psycho-babble. And last but not least, I choose not to talk about this anymore."

"If that's the way you want it," Anne replied, not at all chastened. "What are you doing this weekend?"

"Tomorrow I'm looking at condominiums."

"If I promise to keep my opinions to myself, can I come with you?"

Paulette put down the spoon and lowered her chin, easing the tightness in her neck. "Actually, I'd appreciate your opinion about real estate."

"Thanks for the vote of confidence, but Ben's the expert in the family. He knows construction inside out."

"Bring him along," said Paulette.

Anne suggested they have brunch at The Ovens of Brittany before they went house-hunting. "To fortify ourselves," she said. "What time would you like us to come by for you?"

"Why don't I pick you up?" Paulette replied. "It'll give me a chance to test-drive my new car."

"So you finally got round to buying one," said Anne. "Are you sure you're ready for that much commitment?"

Paulette smiled weakly. "These days, Annie, I'm not sure of anything."

IT WAS A MISTAKE going house-hunting with the Gallaghers. They started the expedition with a list of ten prospects: six condos, two duplexes and two houses. Three of the properties they merely drove by, and of the remaining seven, five were clearly unsuitable. They were too large or too small, too quaint or too bland. Anne deplored the floor plans, the layout of the kitchens, the lack of closet space. Ben pointed out slow drains, inadequate insulation and dry rot.

Anne liked the sixth place, and Ben declared it structurally sound. Paulette liked it too, but the financing was an insurmountable drawback. "I'd rather have a warranty deed than a land contract," she said. "That balloon payment's a killer."

All three of them liked the seventh place. It was convenient, airy and spacious, with enough personal touches to give it character and ample storage room. What was more, the price was right. Paulette was on the brink of making an offer when Anne remarked, "This reminds me of your old condo."

"Me too," said Ben. "Didn't there used to be a landfill hereabouts?"

Paulette couldn't get out of there fast enough, despite Anne's protest that lightning didn't strike twice and Ben's observation that she was throwing out the baby with the bathwater.

She dropped the Gallaghers at their house, declining their invitation to stay for supper.

"Hang in there," Ben told her. "There's always next weekend."

"Ben's right," said Anne. "You can't expect to find what you're looking for the first time out."

It was half-past eight when Paulette got home. She trudged upstairs, footsore and dejected, wondering if the whole idea of buying a place was a mistake. Maybe she'd been too hasty, giving up the sublet.

She wasn't hungry, but forced herself to eat a peanut butter sandwich while she watched Christopher Lee terrorize the peasants of Transylvania.

The sandwich left a bitter aftertaste. It sat in her stomach like lead. After he had dispatched the first few victims, Count Dracula's lethal charm began to fade.

Paulette went to bed early that night, and before she turned in, she reconnected the phone.

The studio had never been so lonely.

Her life had never seemed so empty.

She had never missed Jonathan more.

AN ARTICLE ABOUT the Helping Hands fund-raiser appeared in Sunday's *State Journal*. In addition to a history of the organization and an outline of its services, there were group photos of the bachelors who would be auctioned. Paulette was surprised to see Alan Pierson among them.

She scanned the photos until she found Jonathan. He was the only one in his group who wasn't smiling, and his soberness set him apart. He looked anything but charitable and undeniably sexy; as if he might steal a kiss or break a heart and never give a damn.

Paulette imagined women all over Dane County swooning over his picture and itching to reform him, whether he needed it or not.

The next morning her clock radio woke her with a rendition of "My Funny Valentine," and the announcement:

> He's handsome! He's successful! And he's available—at the right price! If you'd like to spend an evening with one of Madison's most eligible bachelors, don't miss the first annual Bachelor Auction, February 13th at the Sheraton Ballroom. The gavel goes down at 7:30 p.m. Twenty lucky ladies will win dream dates with the city's most sought-after men. Proceeds go to Helping Hands, so be there! Bid fast, bid often, and the man of your dreams could be yours.

On her way to work that day, Paulette suffered through the same message on her car radio. That evening *Newscene 15* featured an interview with the local coordinator of Helping Hands. By Tuesday Madison was inundated with TV spots, bumper stickers and billboards, and by Wednesday, the auction was the talk of the town.

There was no escaping it, even at Shorewood. After all, their very own basketball coach was involved.

In the registrar's office, the stenos gathered round the coffee machine and made plans to reserve a table at the Sheraton, and some enterprising undergraduates had started a pool. The faculty, students and office personnel, even the powers that be in administration, were placing bets on how high the bidding on Alan Pierson would run.

Paulette watched all this with mixed emotions. She sympathized with the plight of the farmers, but how could she forget about Jonathan when his picture was plastered on the backs of the Metro buses?

On Friday night she visited Ronnie's dressing room after the recital, and found herself face-to-face with yet another auction poster.

"This is the last straw," she muttered. Only Ronnie's steady appraisal kept her from tearing the poster down.

"What's wrong with it, Paulette?"

"It's—it's *corny*, that's all. The height of bad taste."

"Do you really think so?"

"Don't you?"

"Nope. I kind of like it myself. I think it's a great picture of Jonathan."

"But this whole media blitz is so tacky!"

Ronnie studied the poster and shook her head. "I don't get it. Why are you so upset? It's all in fun and it's for a good cause. It's not as if the publicity's hurting anyone."

"It's hurting me!" Paulette cried. "I can't bear the thought of Jack going out with another woman."

Ronnie gave her a measuring glance. "Who says he has to?"

Chapter Twenty

"It would be nice if he were taller, but looks aren't everything."

"You are so right. That's why I'm going for bachelor number twelve."

"Isn't he offering the dinner cruise on the Mississippi?"

"Yes, and he's adorable."

"I'm partial to bachelor number seven myself."

"What's he offering?"

"The Milwaukee Symphony and dinner at Mader's."

"Well, I prefer the riverboat."

Paulette bounced up and down on her tiptoes and looked over Anne's shoulder, straining to get a clearer view of the ballroom. She caught a glimpse of a podium flanked by TV cameras and a runway ringed by tables, but the swarm of women ahead of her prevented her seeing anything more.

"I hope Ronnie got here early enough to save us seats."

"I'm sure she did," said Anne.

Paulette wedged her wrist up and checked her watch. It was almost seven-thirty. "What's happening, Annie? Can you see? Why is the line moving so slowly?"

"They're setting up more tables—oh, look! There's Ronnie."

Paulette stretched as tall as she was able and peered in the direction Anne was waving. She saw the glitter of jewelry and a sea of avid faces turned toward the podium, but she couldn't spot Ronnie.

"Six, please. Six," called the man taking tickets.

The crowd thinned long enough for Paulette to remove her ticket from her evening bag, then an elbow dug into her spine and the line surged forward.

"This catalogue's better than Spiegel's."

"But where are they hiding the merchandise?"

"With this big a turnout, it's gotta be a seller's market. How high do you suppose the bidding will run?"

"Three, please. Three," called the ticket taker.

The babble of voices was deafening; the clash of perfumes sickening. Hemmed in on all sides, Paulette had barely enough room to breathe, and all she could do was endure slow suffocation and wait for her turn to be seated. Ahead of her loomed the overcrowded ballroom; behind her the line had mushroomed halfway down the staircase to the lobby.

"They'll never fit us all at the tables," she said.

"Relax," Anne replied. "I heard they're installing television monitors in the banquet room."

"Five, please. Five." The ticket taker lowered the rope that cordoned off the doorway, and another group funneled past the barricade.

"We're next," said Anne, stepping into the breach.

Paulette lagged behind, watching the ticket man usher his charges to a table on the far side of the runway. Now that her view was less obstructed, she saw that mirrored walls at either end of the ballroom reflected an infinity of auction-goers.

"Oh, God, I can't go through with this," she groaned. "I'm the last person on earth Jack would want to see."

"He'll be delighted," said Anne. She tugged at Paulette's arm, but Paulette resisted.

"He'll be furious," she said. "I hurt his feelings. I hurt his pride—"

"And this is the perfect opportunity to make amends." The ticket taker had turned and was making his way back to the door. They were running out of time. "Listen, Paulette, you can't back out now. I didn't want to tell you this, but Jonathan's expecting you to be here."

"That's impossible, Annie. How could he find out?"

"I told him. I've been keeping him posted the last two weeks."

"You mean you've been spying on me?"

"It was in your best interest," said Anne. "And Jonathan, poor guy, was beside himself. He had to know what you were up to."

"If he was that desperate, why didn't he call me?"

"Because I advised him not to."

"Of all the rotten, sneaky, underhanded—! How could you interfere like that? I thought you were my friend."

"I don't blame you for being angry," said Anne. "I wouldn't blame you if you never spoke to me again, but what else was I to do? You kept looking at condos and insisting you never wanted to see him again."

"But I was just blowing off steam. I didn't mean it."

"I know you didn't, but I wasn't sure you knew it, so I told Jonathan to wait till you were ready to patch things up."

"Six, please. Table for six."

"We already have a table." Anne handed the man her ticket and dived into the ballroom the moment he lowered the rope, towing a dumbstruck Paulette after her.

"Six, please. Six," the man repeated, snagging Paulette's ticket as she scurried by.

She followed Anne blindly, squeezing through the crowd, taking the shortest route to Ronnie's table.

"Was Ben part of the conspiracy?" Paulette inquired. "Did he deliberately talk me out of buying that condo?"

"We both did," Anne admitted. "While I'm at it, I may as well confess, I thought his comment about the landfill was particularly inspired."

"What about Ronnie? Is she in on it, too?"

"What do you think?"

"I think she is."

Anne flashed her a cheeky smile. "So what are you going to do about it?"

"Nothing," said Paulette. "Absolutely nothing. I'm in a forgiving mood." She was grateful to her friends. Without their intervention, her vanity might have cost her Jonathan.

By now they were nearing their table. Ronnie sprang to her feet. "Isn't this something?" she caroled. "Didn't I tell you the place would be packed?"

"You certainly did, but we made it," said Anne.

"Just in time," Paulette added.

Even as she sank into her chair the houselights dimmed. Silence filled the room, startling in its completeness. The air seemed electric with anticipation as spotlights danced along the runway and focused on the podium, where the Helping Hands coordinator was testing the microphone, preparing to start the festivities.

A smattering of applause greeted him, and the applause became more general when he promised to keep his remarks brief.

He welcomed the audience and thanked them for supporting Helping Hands. He expressed the wish that they would find the evening entertaining, and then said, "Everyone who paid to participate in the auction should have a program and a paddle. You'll find the terms of payment printed inside the back cover of your program. The paddles are to facilitate the sale. Instead of calling out your bids, hold up your paddle, and our auctioneer will acknowledge your bid by referring to the number on the paddle.

"And now, without further ado, I'd like to introduce our auctioneer—"

An enthusiastic round of applause drowned the rest of the introduction, and a dapper, mustachioed man stepped onto the podium. He shook hands with the coordinator, placed a stack of note cards on the lectern, and a hush settled over the audience as he polished his eyeglasses, then put them on.

"Ladies, may I direct your attention to the first item in the catalogue."

He pointed his gavel toward the velvet portieres at the head of the runway, and a cheer rose from the crowd as bachelor number one made his entrance.

"What a hunk!" Ronnie whispered, but even her whisper carried to the man onstage.

He grinned, acknowledging the compliment, and a collective sigh gusted through the room. Paddles flew up before the auctioneer called for bids. At every table would-be buyers scooted forward until they were sitting on the edges of their chairs, but as the bidding got underway, Paulette settled back and leafed through her program.

Jonathan's picture was on page eighteen, which meant a two-to three-hour wait before he'd put in an appearance. She poured a glass of white wine from the carafe at the center of the table, and sipped it to help pass the time.

"Two-fifty, do I hear three?" chanted the auctioneer.

Paulette crossed her legs, smoothed her skirt over her knees, and wondered if Jonathan would notice her new dress.

"Three hundred once. Three hundred twice. Fair warning—Sold to buyer number sixty-three for three hundred dollars."

The auctioneer pounded his gavel and the winning bidder squealed and ran onto the ramp to say hello to her purchase.

Paulette stole a glance at her watch and wondered whether Jonathan felt as anxious as she did.

Her anxiety grew as the evening continued and the bidding ran higher. Bachelor number eight sold for seven hundred twenty-five dollars; number sixteen went for nine hundred.

Paulette read the conditions of payment on the back cover of her program—and the handwriting on the wall. Attending the auction had been a last-minute decision. She hadn't established her credentials with the committee, so her commercial checking account was useless. And since she hadn't bothered to replace her credit cards after the fire, all the cash she had with her was the thousand dollars in traveler's checks she'd purchased at the bank that morning, and the spare change at the bottom of her purse.

While bachelor number seventeen paraded on the ramp, she consulted Anne and Ronnie. "If I start bidding and have to drop out, it'll make matters worse," she said. "Jack will be convinced I don't care for him at all. Maybe I should leave."

"You can't leave!" said Anne.

"Don't worry about money," said Ronnie. "We'll take care of it."

"Sold for nine hundred fifty dollars," the auctioneer shouted, and the audience applauded and cheered.

Please, God, Paulette petitioned. *I've tried to be a good person, and I haven't asked for anything since Chatty Cathy. If you'll let me have Jonathan, I'll never ask you for anything else.*

She blotted beads of perspiration off her forehead with her cocktail napkin, and kept her eyes on the runway as the auctioneer directed the crowd's attention to item number eighteen.

All the other bachelors had worn tuxedos. Jonathan wore one too, but he had taken off the jacket. He carried it hooked over his shoulder when he walked through the curtains, and he looked so handsome, so appealing, so *dear* that she couldn't imagine why she'd ever been foolish enough to suggest he was replaceable.

Her hands felt clammy. Her heart did crazy flip-flops against her ribs. She was nervous for him, but he seemed totally at ease as he strolled along the runway. Somebody whistled, and he assumed a bodybuilder's stance and flexed his biceps, grinning as if to say, "This is all in fun, ladies. I don't take it seriously."

The audience loved it. In unison, hundreds of women screamed their appreciation, and when Jonathan removed the carnation from his buttonhole and tossed the flower to the crowd, he brought them to their feet.

He strode along one side of the ramp and made his way back along the other, stopping now and again to wave or flirt or throw a kiss. One blue-haired lady reached out to touch him as he went by, and he knelt down and kissed her hand.

The crowd went wild, and Paulette's heart sank. With each endearing gesture she wanted him more—and his price shot higher, farther beyond her reach.

The auctioneer pounded his gavel and paddles went up all over the room, her own among them. The bidding started at three hundred dollars, and as it progressed, she was acutely aware of Ronnie and Anne circulating among nearby tables, conducting hurried conferences.

"Five hundred, do I have five-fifty?"

Paulette held her paddle higher.

"Six, do I have six-fifty?"

Jonathan sat at the end of the ramp, urging the bidding on.

"Eight, do I have eight-fifty?"

Paulette caught Jonathan's gaze. A slow grin illumined his face. He winked at her, and women who had dropped out of the bidding dropped into it again.

"Nine-fifty, do I have a thousand?"

Ronnie and Anne rushed back to Paulette, wads of bills clutched in their hands.

"Eleven-fifty, do I have eleven seventy-five?"

"Go for it," Ronnie instructed Paulette. "There's another two hundred here."

"And I have some money in my purse," said Anne.

"I do, too," said Ronnie, glancing around the table. "Anyone else want to contribute?"

"Twelve hundred, do I have twelve twenty-five?"

A hasty count revealed the ladies at her table had kicked in another fifty dollars. Paulette upended her evening bag, and Anne and Ronnie searched the contents for coins.

"Twelve hundred, do I have—?"

Paulette jumped to her feet. "Twelve hundred fifty-one dollars and eighty-six cents!" she shouted.

The crowd roared its approval, and while the auctioneer concluded the sale, Paulette made a dash for Jonathan. He held out both hands to her, and when she reached him, he pulled her onto the runway and into his arms.

He kissed her once for the benefit of the television cameras, then again, more thoroughly, for his own benefit. Between kisses she said, "I've decided to take you up on your offer, Jack."

"You'll move in with me?"

Paulette smiled, making light of her feelings. "I can't afford not to," she confessed. "I took your advice and invested my insurance settlement in a mutual fund. After I pay off Helping Hands, I won't be able to pay next month's rent."

"It's a good thing you have an understanding landlord," said Jonathan.

He would have kissed her a third time, but one of the newsmen called out, "Your bio says you're a financial analyst, Jon. Do you consider yourself a sound investment?"

The audience laughed, and Jonathan replied, "You'll have to ask the lady."

"The ball's in your court, Miss D'Amboise. Rumor has it you and Jon have dated a few—"

"Yes, we have," Jonathan interrupted.

The newsman held the microphone closer to Paulette. "Just between you and me, is Jon a good investment?"

For the first time since he'd walked on stage, Jonathan seemed uneasy. Paulette knew he expected her to respond the way she usually did to leading questions, with a flippant "Do prunes have wrinkles?" or something equally obnoxious. Looking at the newsman's fatuous smile, she was tempted to reply just that way. But then she looked at Jonathan.

"Jon's the best," she said quietly, and her sincerity was obvious. No one, including Jonathan, had any doubt that she meant it.

LATER THAT NIGHT, in the privacy of his living room, Jonathan chided her for her extravagance.

"Don't worry," she said. "I intend to get my money's worth."

"And I intend to see that you do."

He took her into his arms, lifting her to her tiptoes and fitting her to himself while he kissed her forehead, her eyelids, her temples, and as his lips moved across her cheek to her mouth, she exhaled on a sigh that blended her breath with his.

Her mouth was soft and sensual, her body warm and desirous, but he had waited so long for this moment that kissing her was not enough. Holding her was not enough. He wanted to touch her, wanted to slide his hands beneath the shimmering folds of her dress and stroke the warm, willing flesh the fabric concealed.

Eagerness made his hands clumsy as he fumbled with the zipper, and when it gave way he nuzzled the bodice aside and found the lush curve of her breast. He sampled the yearning nipple through the lacy scrap of her bra, teasing it with his tongue until his assault on her senses made her head spin. She wrapped her arms about him, urging him nearer.

"How am I doing so far, love?"

She rubbed her face against his hair, savoring its thick, springy texture. "You're priceless, Jack. Absolutely priceless."

His mouth settled hungrily over hers, and even as she returned the kiss she was tingling with anticipation. Somehow he had freed the fastener on her bra and now her panties were joining her other garments on the floor. In the next instant, without relinquishing his claim on her mouth, Jonathan swept her up in his arms.

She felt giddy, almost as if she were floating, until she felt the scratchiness of a blanket against her back. She realized that she was lying on his bed, and she watched through half-closed eyes while he stripped off his clothes.

How beautiful he was! How fine and strong and virile! She saw his arousal and held out her arms to him, and when he sank down beside her and caught her in his arms once more, the last remnant of doubt vanished in the wild magic of his lovemaking.

He told her how lovely she was. He called her his darling, his sweetheart, his love. He courted her with lingering kisses and with tantalizing caresses, and seemed to know just what to say and exactly where his touch would create the most delicious sensations. He adored her with his hands and with his mouth and finally drew her into an embrace so deep she might never escape.

But she no longer wanted to escape. Not when she had him.

She wound her arms and legs about him and ran her hands across his back, clinging to him so fiercely that her fingernails raked his shoulders. She strained against him, pressing her mouth to the throbbing hollow at the base of his throat, relishing the clean salty taste of him, inhaling the hot earthy scent of his skin, and when she felt the fluid pulsations that signaled release, she felt as if she were absorbing him through her pores.

Sometime after midnight, passion spent, they fell asleep in each other's arms, and when Paulette woke on Sunday morning, she still felt as if she were part of Jonathan.

Her lips tasted of him. His scent clung to her skin. It was as if their souls had bonded, and she knew that in some mystical but very real way, Jonathan would be with her always.

Chapter Twenty-One

Sunday evening came too soon. Jonathan gave Paulette the Chatty Cathy doll before he left for the airport. "She'll keep you company while I'm gone," he said.

Paulette was stunned. "She's as adorable as I remember, but wherever did you find her?"

Jonathan told her about his dinner with Dina Zhenkov and his chance discovery of the doll in the shop window. "She looked pretty sad," he said. "I knew I had to rescue her, and when I told Dina about the very special lady I was buying Cathy for, she offered to make her a new wardrobe."

With infinite care, Paulette fluffed the ruffles on the doll's pinafore. *Someday I'll give her to my daughter,* she thought, and an image flashed into her mind of a redheaded moppet with Jonathan's eyes. Her voice broke as she said, "You shouldn't have gone to all that trouble."

"It was no trouble. Not as long as you like her."

"*Like* her?" Paulette shifted the doll to one arm and threw the other around his neck. "Oh, Jack, no one ever gave me a present that meant more to me. No one ever will. I feel as if I'm seven again, and it's Christmas morning, and you—well, you're Santa Claus!"

She gave Jonathan an ecstatic hug, and he folded her into his arms.

"I love you, Paulette."

A stillness overcame her. For perhaps half a minute, she hardly dared breathe. And then she pulled away so that she could see his face.

"And I love you, Jack Day."

The tenderness in her smile told him how much, and when Chatty Cathy echoed the sentiment, he couldn't help grinning.

"God, I'm happy!" he said.

"Me too," said Paulette. So happy, she didn't know whether to laugh or cry.

The next six weeks were the most fulfilling she'd ever known—and the most trying. While winter turned to spring and Jonathan concluded his business on the West Coast, she spent her days in limbo, waiting for the weekends. Then, for the forty-eight hours he was home, she stopped waiting and started living.

Jonathan never talked about the future. He never made plans beyond the next weekend, and neither of them mentioned what might happen in April, when their two-month trial period was over. But Jonathan seemed content, and Paulette realized she should be, too.

It gave her great joy to see his face first thing in the morning and last thing at night, and just being with him made their time together glorious. Whether they went out on the town, visited friends or spent the weekend quietly alone, every Saturday and Sunday was like a holiday. And every time they made love was like their *last* time—as if they might never make love again.

She should have been satisfied, but it wasn't enough. Weekends weren't enough. Two months weren't enough. Two years with Jonathan wouldn't be enough to show him how much she cared. She couldn't put a deadline on her need for him; couldn't measure her feelings in terms of time.

At the end of March, out of desperation, she enrolled in some classes at the Y: modern dance for fun, karate to improve her body, creative writing to improve her mind. But the following day brought a change of heart about her self-improvement course. She skipped the evening's classes in favor of stopping by Orchard Manor Nursing Home.

When she walked into the lobby, the first person she saw was Henry Gough, speeding along the corridor in his wheelchair with Miss Costigan, the night supervisor, in hot pursuit.

Miss Costigan saw Paulette and stopped to catch her breath. "We've missed you, Paulette. Where have you been keeping yourself?"

"She's got a boyfriend," said Henry. "Fine-lookin' young feller. Came in with her at Christmas."

"That's right," said Paulette. "His name's Jonathan Day."

Henry rolled his chair closer and cast a pointed look at her left hand. "Ain't married yet, I see."

"No, not yet."

"How come?"

"Henry!" the supervisor scolded. "I believe you're wanted in the solarium."

"You don't need to run interference, Miss Costigan," said Paulette. "Henry and I have an understanding. He asks any question he wants, and I answer any I want."

Miss Costigan looked doubtful, but after hesitating briefly she gestured as if she were washing her hands of the matter, and bustled away down the hall.

"Thought she'd never leave," said Henry, swiveling his chair toward Paulette. "What can I do for you?"

"If you've got a few minutes, I wondered if maybe we could talk."

"Hell's bells! I got nothin' but time."

"You've got experience, Henry."

"You better believe it. Eighty-five years' worth. But there's a heap of stuff I've forgotten." He tapped one finger to his temple. "Memory's not what it used to be."

"But there are some things a person never forgets."

Henry subjected her to a shrewd glance. "This have anything to do with that young man of yours?"

"It has everything to do with him."

"Well then, toots, you've come to the right place. But why me? You must have friends you could talk to."

"None with your wisdom."

"If you're lookin' for advice, what's wrong with your folks?"

Paulette averted her gaze. "They're biased."

"You want someone impartial?"

She nodded.

"Someone honest?"

"Yes," she replied. "More than anything else, I'm relying on your honesty."

Henry gave the wheels on his chair a decisive spin. "Let's go to the lounge. No one's there this hour of the night. They're all watchin' Cosby. We'll have some of that decaffeinated slop they call coffee—my treat—and you can tell me all about it."

For the next two hours, Paulette talked and Henry listened. Slowly at first, then in a rush, the confidences came pouring out. After a couple of false starts she began at the beginning, with her parents, her sister, herself.

"All my life I've seen myself as a certain kind of person," she told him. "I've thought of Nicole and myself as carbon copies—extroverted, adventurous and reluctant to form attachments. But since I met Jack, I've discovered I'm not that way at all. At least, not completely. But I'm afraid that may be what he wants—"

She told Henry quite a lot about Jonathan, just for the joy of talking about him. But mostly she talked about love.

She said, "I told Jack I love him, and it's true. I do love him. But the problem is, I've never been in love before, and I'm not sure how to show it. My mother, for instance, expresses her love by doing things for people. I guess nurturing is the word that describes her best. She might complain and criticize, but she's always eager to help. There have been times when she's done things for me I'd rather she wouldn't do, and when she's crossed the line, I haven't always been tactful in the way I've declined her assistance, but it's only recently that I've begun to see why she takes this as a rejection."

"How about your dad?" asked Henry.

"He's an idealist. He tends to express his love in less tangible ways. It's as if he wants to create this perfect world for his family to live in—"

"The trouble with that is creating perfect people," said Henry.

"Please don't get the wrong impression," said Paulette. "My father's tolerant. He's very forgiving, but he's also deeply, *deeply* hurt when his children don't subscribe to his beliefs."

Henry tugged at the stubble on his chin. "Tell me about your boyfriend. Does he treat you right?"

"Oh, yes. Jack's one in a million. He accepts me just as I am—or at least the way I used to see myself. He thinks I want freedom, and that's what he's giving me."

"Only now you've got it, you want somethin' else."

Paulette sighed. "When you put it that way, it seems awfully selfish."

"It's human," said Henry. "No more, no less. But let's get down to the nub of it. Exactly what is it you're askin'?"

"Well, what I'd really like to know is how I can convince Jack I love him."

Henry reacted with a sly double take and a hoot of laughter. "You're the tassel on the corn, toots! I mean, you are some piece of work. In the first place, your face lights up whenever you mention Jack's name, so I doubt he needs any convincin'. In the second place, love isn't somethin' you prove, it's somethin' you *share*. And in the third place, instead of wastin' your time with me, you oughta be sayin' all this to Jack."

Henry was right! She knew he was. She felt it in her bones. His solution was so basic, she marveled that she hadn't seen it from the start.

On her way home that night, she resolved to tell Jack about her conversation with Henry at the very first opportunity. She got her chance the following Saturday, and although baring her soul did not come naturally, she stuck to her resolution.

She began by asking, "Did you ever hear the story of the fisherman's wife?"

Jonathan said he had.

"Well, that's how I feel, like the fisherman's wife. She does one good deed for a flounder, and in return he grants her a wish. He turns her rundown hovel into a neat little cottage. But is she satisfied?"

Jonathan cleared his throat. His face was pale in the lamplight. "More to the point, are you?"

Paulette admitted she wasn't, and his pallor increased. "Tell me what's wrong," he said. "We can work it out."

"Can we, Jack? I'm not sure. Maybe the idea of a trial period was a mistake."

Jonathan took her hand. She could feel him trembling. "If you're feeling pressured, I'll back off. If you need more space, you can use the studio. If you want more time to yourself, say the word and it's yours."

Was he trying to get rid of her? She couldn't look at him. She lowered her gaze and spoke in an anguished whisper. "What if I want more time with you?"

"Whatever you want, sweetheart, all you have to do is ask."

"But what if I want more than two months?"

"It's yours." Jonathan's arms went around her and hauled her close. "This is where you belong, Paulette. Here. With me. For as long as we both shall live."

"Always?" she said.

"Always," he replied without hesitation. "I'm asking you to marry me."

Paulette thought the proposal over for all of a minute. She thought of Henry Gough saying "I told you so," and her father performing the ceremony. She thought of Carl Bemis walking her down the aisle, and her mother dancing at the reception—maybe with Sergei Zhenkov. She pictured Nicole and the Gallaghers in their wedding finery, and Jonathan in his, and herself in white lace, radiant with happiness. She envisioned her father's church filled with flowers and candlelight, and it was wonderful and romantic.

The idea of meeting Jonathan's parents brought on an attack of cold feet, but the thought that Jonathan would be there to warm them made her shiver with excitement.

"Do you suppose Ronnie would sing 'My Funny Valentine' at the wedding?"

"If that's the song you'd like, I guarantee it," said Jonathan.

With that settled, Paulette accepted. How could she refuse? "Do you realize, spread over fifty years of marriage, you'll have cost me only two dollars a month?"

"And think of the dividends," said Jonathan.

Paulette could think of little else.

The first bonus that came to mind was that she loved Jonathan. The second, even more astounding, was that he loved her. The third was that she liked the Paulette she saw reflected in his eyes.

"Know what?" she murmured. "First thing tomorrow, I'm going to burn my address book."

"You don't have to do that, Paulette. Not on my account."

"I know I don't have to, but I've outgrown the book. I don't need it anymore. And that's why I want to—"

Jonathan cradled her head against his shoulder and silenced her with a kiss. She felt his lips curve into a smile as he whispered, "In that case, sweetheart, I'm sure Doris Day would approve."

acting job and start living life for herself. But driving Mouse cross-country brings Suzanne more than just freedom. It brings her handsome young Wyoming cowboy Billy Blue. Now that she's finally on her own, is Suzanne ready for love?

#259 HARVEST THE SUN by Judith Arnold

For Abbie Jarvis, life in the big city was worth every sacrifice. But when prosecuting an emotional case leaves her needing R and R, she retreats to her small northern California hometown. In need of a friend, she walks straight into the arms of T.J. Hillyard, local hero. Like T.J., Abbie had tasted the glory she yearned for—but was it enough? Or had what she'd been looking for always been right in her own backyard?

#260 CRY FOR THE MOON by Anne Stuart

Marielle Brandt didn't have much choice after she was suddenly widowed and left alone to raise her two small children. The only legacy from her husband was Farnum's Castle, a run-down apartment house in Chicago. The building housed some eccentric inhabitants, including two psychics and a warlock—but it also was home to Simon Zebriskie, resident helper and late-night DJ. It seemed to Marielle a most unlikely place to fall in love, but how could she deny Simon's powerful sensuality?

Four believable American Romance heroines…four contemporary American women just like you…by four of your favorite American Romance authors.

Don't miss these special stories. Enjoy the fifth-anniversary celebration of Harlequin American Romance.

SPECIAL ANNIVERSARY ISSUE ★ 5 YEAR ★ SPECIAL ANNIVERSARY ISSUE

AR5A-2